CINDY DORMINY

The Foster Wife

Helping Men Find Their Forever Homes

The Foster Wife
Red Adept Publishing, LLC
104 Bugenfield Court
Garner, NC 27529
https://RedAdeptPublishing.com/

---

1.   http://StreetlightGraphics.com

To all the foster pups out there, especially Tapas and Fancy

CHAPTER ONE
Amelia

Sweat trickles down the side of Jonathan Franklin Rothchild's adorable baby face as he kneels in front of me. From his suit pocket, he fishes out a three-carat Asscher cut diamond ring in a platinum setting.

That's his grandmother's ring!

"Amelia Day, will you marry me?"

I clasp my hands over my heart and squeal. "Yes."

I fall into his arms, and he swings me around in a circle.

When my feet hit the ground, I stare at the ring one more time before handing it back to him. "That was perfect. You passed the final test." After I scribble my signature on his certificate of completion, I turn it around to show him. "Congratulations. I think you are one hundred percent ready to meet your future wife."

Jonathan's mouth turns up into a bashful grin as he takes the certificate in his shaking hands. "Really? Are you sure? Because if you don't think I'm ready—"

"I don't sign off on a client until I know he has made a significant change and has had enough time to create new habits. You were one of the easier ones."

Compared to some, he was a piece of cake. Unlike Jonathan, my clients before him, the Baker twins, tried to trip each other up at every stage, so working with this executive sweetheart was a breeze. Herding cats would be simpler than managing those two heathens, especially at the same time. *What was I thinking? Oh yeah. Money.*

Jonathan is now everything a girl would ever want in a husband. He's kind and giving, and he breezed through the steps in record time. I think he's my best client so far. No more fleas. Hello, marriage.

I look around the penthouse apartment I've shared with Jonathan for the last two months, thinking back to how much work it took to get him ready to find his forever mate. He started as a recluse with a large bank account, falling prey to every gold digger in the city, but now he's a confident yet sensitive and successful bachelor. I beam with pride thinking about his transformation.

"Any girl would be lucky to snag you."

He blushes. "Aw, I bet you say that to all your clients."

"Only when I mean it." I wag my index finger in his face. "Do you remember that one specific item that kept you from passing earlier?"

He counts off on his hands as he mumbles under his breath. His shoulders slump. "Parasites. They got me every time, didn't they?"

I pat his shoulder. "Eventually, you figured it out. And now you know the warning signs. The last few times we showcased you at the bar, you did really well at keeping the women away who were only interested in you for your money. That's your biggest hurdle. You have to focus on your—"

"Forever home," he says, finishing my sentence.

With a heavy sigh, I hold out my hand to shake his. I am both elated and sad this day has come. He is such a nice guy. I almost broke one of my rules—be nice but not too friendly. The men who hire me are clients, and I must keep it professional every step of the way.

"I wish you the best."

"Thank you so much. Your payment should be in your Venmo account by the end of the day."

With one hand, Jonathan wheels my luggage, and with the other, he drags my clunky trifold display board down the hallway as I grab my purse, laptop bag, and dog carrier. We take the elevator down to the main floor in silence. Living in such a luxury condo has been amazing, definitely my favorite location. My clients usually live in run-down apartments, and one even resided in his mother's basement. I shiver thinking of some of the men who never completed my program, or worse, those who never made it past the background check. But for the most part, I have an amazing track record for successfully converting perpetual bachelors into serious husband material. I love knowing I prepare them for a fulfilling life with someone special. Prepping men for marriage is what I do.

Jonathan loads my luggage into his limo and gives me one last hug. "Thanks, Amelia. You've changed me in more ways than I ever imagined."

Pride washes over me as I give him a bashful shrug. "That's my job."

He places a stack of cash into my hand, enough to at least let me make the minimum payment on one of my bills. "Just a little tip to tide you over until you get your next client."

I stare down at the pile of crisp hundred-dollar bills as I blink back tears. "Jonathan, I can't take this."

"If you don't, I'll add it to the amount I pay you online. Your choice."

He's so ready for a committed relationship.

As I settle into the back seat, I wave one last time to Jonathan. I'll miss him, but he doesn't need my services anymore.

"Did you two break up?" Mr. Cantrell, the driver, asks as he pulls out into traffic.

"Oh, no. We weren't a couple. He was my client."

"Is that what they call it these days?"

A heat flushes over my neck and face. "It wasn't like that at all. I don't sleep with my clients. That would be unethical and against my strict policies."

The driver chuckles. "Why aren't you married?"

Mr. Cantrell and I have had many conversations over the last two months. I think he's asked me that same question at least a dozen times.

I force a smile. "And miss out on helping other men? No way. This is way more satisfying." *Keep telling yourself that.*

I am one step closer to having the money I need. As long as I can hold off the loan officer just a bit longer, everything will be *pawsitively* perfect.

My sister opens the door to her fancy house, saving me from another scolding from her awful neighbor. I scoot inside with Dolly in her carrier and let out a sigh.

"Is Mrs. Kingsman harassing you again?"

I nod. "She hates me."

"No, but you have to keep Dolly on a leash. It's a 'covenant' and very important to her. Trust me, I hear about it every time you open the door and let Dolly loose."

I open my mouth to tell her how stupid Mrs. Kingsman's covenant is, but Dorothy holds up a hand to stop my words.

"I know, but you know her."

When the smells of baked bread and finger paint invade my olfactory system, I forget all about her cranky neighbor. My niece and nephew toddle over to me, and I scoop little Zoey into my arms while Tucker peers into the dog carrier.

"I missed you. You've gotten so big since I saw you last."

Dorothy rolls her eyes. "You saw her two days ago."

"I know." I cover Zoey's face with kisses, and she lets out the cutest squeal. "Two days is too long. I'm sure she grew at least an inch since then." I hold her at arm's length and nod. "At least two inches taller."

Tucker wraps his arm around my leg while I shuffle toward the living room.

"Are you staying with us?" he asks.

"Yep, until my next client is arranged."

"Can I get a puppy?"

I glance over at Dorothy, who mouths "no" to me. "You know you can stop by and play with the puppies where I volunteer. Those dogs always need some extra attention before they are adopted. But remember what I told you. The right dog at the right time."

Tucker sticks out his bottom lip in the most adorable pout. "But the last time I was there, I *did* find the right dog."

Dorothy takes Zoey from my arms and places her in the swing. "Honey, he was a Great Dane. You could have ridden him like a horse."

"Duh," Tucker says to his mother, adding an eye roll no teenager could do better.

I ruffle his shaggy hair. "I'll keep my eye out for your perfect dog. In the meantime..."

I open my dog carrier and wait for my cute little mutt to crawl out of her safe space and into the toddler-filled room.

Zoey squirms, trying to extricate herself from the swing when she sees my tiny dog emerge from her carrier.

Dolly sniffs around, scoping out the place. She's pretty used to bouncing from one house to the other, but it's definitely better than her original owner, who traveled nonstop and kenneled the poor pup more days than not.

Tucker reaches for her, but Dorothy snatches Dolly Pawdon before Tucker can grab her tail.

"Be nice." Dorothy nuzzles the little tricolored fur ball. "Hello, sweetie. I missed you."

Dolly's motor rumbled as if she were a cat.

I scratch the back of Dolly's head. "I think she got spoiled living the good life in that penthouse apartment."

Dorothy chuckles. "I would too. But she'll have to come back down to reality and live with the mere mortals for a while."

As I collapse on the couch, Tucker loses interest in me and my dog and picks up a toy truck. While he *vroom vroooms* around our feet, Dorothy asks, "How did this one go?"

"His biggest problem was that he was so gullible. He fell for every trick in the book. Women figure out he's loaded, and they glom on to him. It took a while, but he finally learned to keep them at bay."

"Ah, yes, the parasites. Or was it the fleas or kennel cough?" She giggles. "I seriously can't keep all your dog analogies straight."

While I admit my terminology is a bit weird, it's spot-on. I reply with a shrug. "My system works."

"Jonathan seemed really nice at the family meet-and-greet session. Even Axel didn't scare him away."

The step to ensure a man can handle the gauntlet of a potential wife's family is vital. If a client messes that up, it quite often causes them to relapse, and we have to start again from scratch.

"I figure if my clients can pass through the challenge of my rambunctious family, they can handle any family gatherings in the real world."

She nods as she pets Dolly. "That's true. I still remember when Dax met everyone. I just knew y'all had scared him away."

"And that's why I add that step close to the end, if they get that far."

Dorothy rolls her eyes. "Only *you* would have a job transforming men into husband material."

My jaw drops. "Hey, I have a wonderful track record. Plus, it's a great business. I keep hoping the animal shelter will take me on as a paid employee, but donations are down, and they have a hiring freeze. So it looks like I will be a volunteer for at least another year. It doesn't pay anywhere near what my foster-wife business does, but dogs are always happy to see me, so there's that."

"You could look for a different job. Dax would hire you in a New York minute to be his receptionist."

I don't even try to keep the groan quiet. We've had this conversation about my brother-in-law's company so many times I have lost count. Wearing a pencil skirt while sitting at a desk all day and answering phones sounds as much fun as getting declawed. Plus, I've been down that corporate road before.

"Dax is a great guy, and I'm honored, but you know how much I love working with animals. Those poor babies need me to help them find their *furever* homes. And hopefully, soon I'll have enough money to get out of my mountain of debt."

She holds her hands out in defense, and Dolly Pawdon climbs off her lap and into mine.

After a moment of silence, Dorothy says, "Dax and I would love—"

"Nope. I will not accept your money. I made this mess, and I'll dig my way out. Being able to crash here between clients is more than generous."

She pouts, and I see where Tucker gets his cute expression.

"If you change your mind, we will always be here to help you," she says.

I give her a knowing look. "You know what I make with my clients."

"If I ever run into Bennet, I'm going to give him a piece of my mind."

"Let it go. He didn't force me to try keeping up with his high-society friends."

"He kind of did."

Tucker drives his truck up and down Dorothy's shin, and she doesn't even notice.

I sit taller in my seat and wrack my brain to find a way to steer this conversation away from Bennet and how it led to my being neck-deep in debt. When nothing comes to mind, I say, "This is the fastest way to earn the money, and I'm so close. I can smell it."

Dorothy scrunches her nose. "I think that's a dirty diaper you're smelling."

We chuckle, but Dorothy's smile doesn't reach her eyes, and I know she's reliving my crash-and-burn attempts down the aisle.

Before she can mention it, I say, "I love my life exactly how it's turned out. I don't hold any animosity toward anyone, especially the you-know-whos, and you shouldn't either."

"Whatever you say, sis. I'm at least glad you let Laura run background checks on these guys before you move in with them."

"See? There is one benefit of having a large family." I chuckle. "Our family pretty much has all the major careers covered."

"True." She waves a hand in front of her scrunched face. "I've got to take care of that foul stench coming from the business end of Zoey. You get settled in your room, then maybe we'll take these munchkins on a walk."

Tucker pops up his head. "Can Dolly come too?"

I pull Tucker onto my lap and plant a smooch on his cheek. "Yep. She loves it when you take her for walks."

I release Tucker and drag all my belongings into the spare bedroom Dorothy allows me to use between clients. It should make me sad that everything I own easily fits into one suitcase, but it really doesn't. Life is so much simpler without lots of stuff. Besides, I have everything I need. I have my large, loving family, a great volunteer position, a fantastic business, and the cutest dog in the world. Life is much better without all the material complications. If my exes taught me anything, it's that I will never let anyone squash my joy again, especially a man.

CHAPTER TWO

Phin

If Jay giggles over one of his fiancée's text messages one more time, I think I'm going to hurl all over the BLT sandwich I'm making. The last two months have been nothing but sappy heart emojis and "I love you, too, pookie pie" phone conversations. What's worse is that he gladly cashed in his man card and tries daily to get me to join him on the dark side.

No way.

While I wrap the "Bacon, Lots of bacon, and Top it off with more bacon" sandwich, I wink at the gorgeous blonde waiting for it. She flips her long hair over her shoulder as we have a nonverbal conversation about things that should not be done in my food truck. And if she eats all that pork, I'll eat my guitar picks.

With the sandwich on a plate, I hold my hand out the window. "Here you go, ma'am." On purpose, I let my fingers linger for a moment, making sure they contact hers. "I'm sorry. Can you verify your name? You know... to make sure you get the right sandwich."

Because I wasn't listening.

"Sophia." And on cue, she slips me one of my business cards with what I'm sure includes her phone number.

"Sophia... it's such a beautiful name." I flick my eyes down to the order slip. "Yep. This is yours."

She grins, blinding me with her bleached-white teeth. "I should let you get back to work." Sophia saunters off, putting a little extra spring in her step.

Hubba-hubba. I'm sure I have a new customer for life, and yep, she gave me her phone number. *Sweet.*

Jay clears his throat, breaking my spell. "Orders are piling up, Romeo."

With a grunt, I shove the guitar-pick-shaped card into my front pocket and focus on the next order. We're always extra busy on Wednesdays because the spot in front of the park is walking distance from at least ten different businesses. I shouldn't complain, because we make money hand over fist here. *But Sophia...* I miss her already. But Mr. Griffin needs his Fowl Play sandwich. He's a nice old man who owns the tailor shop around the corner. I usually start making his sandwich when I see him in line because he's one of our most loyal customers, and he orders the exact same meal every time. But Sophia got me distracted, so I was off my game.

"Did you stump Jay today?" I ask.

Mr. Griffin scowls as he looks over his shoulder toward my business partner. "No. That boy knows more music trivia than should be allowed."

I hand him his sandwich. "And what he doesn't know, this guy does." I point both thumbs at myself. "But hey, there's always next time to get your order for free."

With a finger to my mouth to keep him quiet, I slide a few extra pickles onto his basket. It's the least I can do for my favorite customer. He always fake complains about not beating Jay, and I always slip a bonus item to him without my partner catching on.

He points a crooked finger at me as he plays along. "Three years. I've been coming here every Wednesday for three years, and I still haven't been able to out-trivia him or you."

I chuckle because Jay and I are masters at music trivia, and it has been over a year since someone bested us, meaning we haven't shelled out a free meal—other than the weekly freebie unbeknownst to my business partner. It's a brilliant marketing plan to bring in the business, especially in Nashville—Music City, USA. It's certainly better than one of those buy-nine-get-the-tenth-meal-free cards that no one can keep up with.

"See you next week." I wave as Mr. Griffin walks away.

He gives me a backward wave. "Yeah, yeah."

Jay shrugs as he clips another order onto the line and slides it my way. "What can I say? I'm a freak of nature."

"Or maybe just a freak?"

Jay cuts his eyes toward me as he swipes a credit card. "So, is *Sophia* the perfect one for you?"

"Yes, she is, until she isn't."

He hands the credit card back to the customer and clips another order onto the wire. "Too tall or too short? Too blond or not blond enough?"

I wipe the sweat from my forehead with my forearm. "Hey now. It's not my fault women don't live up to my high standards."

Jay snorts as he organizes the bills in the cash register. "Your standards change with the wind. What was wrong with Laurel?"

"She talked too much."

"Renee?"

"Too quiet."

He snorts as he closes the cash drawer. "You're too picky."

"And that's a good thing."

He points a pen at me. "Too picky and too fickle."

"Whatever, man. You stick to your one love, and I'll stick to loving every woman on the planet."

"Speaking of my love, Hazel thinks you could benefit from the program."

I prepare a Let's Be Frank hot dog and slide it onto a paper boat then hand it to the customer. Wiping down my workspace, I say, "I do not need to be in the program. It's stupid. Matthew was already whipped before he did that whole foster-wife thing. And to tell you the truth, having someone live with you when they aren't sleeping with you, training you..." I do a full-body shiver then hold my right hand over my forehead in an L shape. "Loser."

That shuts him up for the time being. When the lunch crowd dies down, Jay flips through the receipts, tallying the sales for the day. "The program does work, by the way. My cousin was a man-ho like you, and you know it."

Placing plastic lids over the condiments to keep them fresh, I check to see which items I need to restock. Matthew used to be as much of a player as I am before he got roped into that ridiculous program. But it will take an act of Congress to get me to settle down. Not happening. I've been burned too many times in the past, and if there's one thing people can say about me, it's that I learn from my mistakes—eventually. Plus, Baxtor men can't commit. It's genetic.

"I think he was just ready to settle down and it was all a coincidence."

Jay shakes his head. "She made him see things differently."

"I like how I see things."

"One day, you'll beg me for her contact info."

I waggle my eyebrows. "Is she cute?"

He huffs. "No—I mean, from the one time I met her, I would consider her very cute—but that's not the point. And Hazel thinks she hung the moon, so there's that. Trust me. You need some fine-tuning."

I let out a huge laugh. "I do not. You make me sound like a fixer-upper."

"If the shoe fits, bro." His brow scrunches, and he mumbles, "Mr. Highfalutin at twelve o'clock."

Glancing up and doing my best not to be obvious, I observe the hoity-toity man who seems to think he's the most important person on the planet. By the way he dresses in the finest business suits but is a complete tightwad when it comes to tips, he's a walking paradox.

He convinces the next person in line to let him go ahead, as usual. It's always a business meeting he's running late for or a very important deal he needs to finalize, something that makes his lunch break much more precious than anyone else's.

Jay clears his throat. "What can I get you today?"

Mr. Highfalutin scans the menu. "Fowl Play, but this time, hold the pickles. The juice messed up my Vardama shirt. It cost me twice as much to get it dry-cleaned."

If he didn't hold the pickle slice above his head like a seal catching a fish, he might not drip it on his shirt, but what do I know?

"Sure thing." Jay rotates the iPad so Mr. Highfalutin can sign the transaction.

Jay slides the order slip toward me on the wire. "You know the drill."

I complete the order and place it on a paper plate, doubling it because I know that's what he will ask for next.

When I hand him his order, he asks, "Could you—"

"Already did."

When he leaves without a thank-you but with half a box of napkins, I say to Jay, "Let me guess. Mr. Highfalutin gave us a twenty-five-cent tip this time."

Jay scoffs. "You wish. Today, it was fifteen cents."

As we watch the businessman eat his sandwich with a triple layer of napkins tucked into the neck of his shirt, I wonder what makes a man like that tick. I know looks can be deceiving, but I bet he's stingy enough to make his girlfriend split the gas money on dates.

I lean out the food truck window in hopes of catching a breeze, but all I get are fumes from the food truck next to us. The Holy Smokers parked too close to us, and their exhaust overpowers their BBQ. Time for a change of subject.

"How did we do in sales today?"

Jay enters some calculations on the iPad and grins. "Real good, Phin. I think next month, I'm going to reserve a spot in the park two days a week. We rake it in when we park here."

A gorgeous redhead sprints by with her fluffy dog trotting beside her. I wave, and she gives me a girly finger wave back.

"I do admit the scenery is way better here than at the Green Hills retirement community."

Jay organizes the cash in the tray and snorts. "The ladies there love you too." In an old woman's voice, he adds, "My my, aren't you a nice slice of pie?"

"I'm just glad I was inside the truck because if I'd had to be out there with them, I am sure I would have been manhandled."

"You could have serenaded them with your latest song."

Heat flames up my neck, and it has nothing to do with the Holy Smokers's fumes. "It's not ready for anyone's ears yet. It would be, though, if you'd loan me your baby." I bat my eyelashes and add, "Paa-weese?"

"Nope. Nobody plays Beatrice except me."

Jay loves his 1970 Fender Stratocaster more than he loves his own mother. Not that I blame him or anything, but I am pretty sure he sleeps with it every night. I certainly would if she was mine. Jay's father was a session player back in the day, and he played this very guitar in a lot of number one hit songs. Only guitar geeks like me and Jay appreciate the guys who make the magic behind the scenes. We both get a little misty-eyed when "Pretty Woman" shows up on our Spotify playlist.

"Come on, man. Let me play the Strat. I'm sure I could knock this new song out before our next gig if I had that ax speaking to me."

He shakes his head as he tallies the lunch sales. "Maybe when you grow up and settle down, I'll let you touch it."

"Not happening, but come on. Ladies love a guy with a guitar like that. Why don't you loan it to me? Then it might help me find the right girl."

Jay rolls his eyes, and I know he didn't buy that line for one second.

"Nope." He shoves the money into a bank bag.

I whimper. "Man, you are cruel."

"You'll do all right. And we don't even have a 'next gig.' We haven't had a single gig. It's just wishful thinking."

"You are the worst business partner, bandmate, and best friend ever. If I had that beauty, I would let *you* borrow it."

He belts out a laugh. "No, you wouldn't. The last time you had anything of value was in high school, when you were the first of us to own a car, and we all know how that ended."

It's not my fault my car accidentally crashed into my mother's mailbox. It never had a chance. I can still hear the *whoosh* from being airborne before landing in the creek beside our house. Mom was so pissed, but I felt like an official member of the Fast and Furious.

"Not funny."

"Oh, it's very funny. But trust me, one day, you'll say 'I told you so' about wanting to get married."

"And one day, you'll let me play your guitar. The ladies will love it. And since you're off the market—"

"Not happening." He shoves money into the bank bag and locks it, then sighs as he shakes his head. "It's not a requirement to live out the most overused rock band cliché. In fact, it's perfectly okay to love one person."

And we are back to that. He just doesn't understand I love my life the way it is. Mom is fine without a partner, and so am I. Besides, Jay knows better than anyone why I am the way I am.

CHAPTER THREE
Amelia

While I prepare the tiny Chihuahua named Tapas for his foster mom, Hazel organizes the bag of supplies. Hazel has seen me in my lowest times, and if she had not suggested I volunteer at the animal shelter, I think I would still be balled up in a fetal position after Ex-Boyfriend Number Three's escapade. A girl can only take so much before she needs a wet canine kiss to make her feel better.

I double-check the immunization records to ensure the little critter is ready for his temporary home. Hazel squeaks the tiny pig toy, making Tapas's ears perk.

"You like that one, don't you, sweetie?"

He does a full-body wag and almost jumps out of my lap watching Hazel toss the squeaky toy into his bag of supplies. Poor little guy. It's not his fault he was part of a hoarding situation, but I'm confident his foster mom will have him socialized, housebroken, and ready for his *furever* home in no time.

"He's so cute. I'm sure once he's on the adoption floor, he'll get a great home." I belt out a line from the song "Puppy Love" as I rub the pup's ears.

Hazel cringes. "You know I think the world of you, but you have to be the most tone-deaf person on the planet."

My mouth drops open. "I'm not *that* bad, am I?"

"Well... do you remember Elaine from *Seinfeld* and how she dances?" She points at me. "That's you but with singing."

"Pfft. We can't all be like my brother. I think he got all the musical genes. Not fair."

"Your talents lie elsewhere." Hazel stares off and chuckles. "Who would have thought you could work your magic on Jay's cousin? That boy is one hundred percent in love. If I hadn't witnessed the transformation myself, I wouldn't have believed it."

"That's why I do it. I knew deep down he was a great guy. All it took was some fine-tuning."

"Oh, Matthew needed more than a little tweak. He was due for a complete overhaul. I'm just lucky Jay didn't need your service. Some men are ready, while others need a nudge."

Her phone makes a woof sound, alerting her to a text message. "Tapas's foster mama is here. Let's go."

I scoop up the supply bag in one hand and nestle little Tapas in the other. Hazel carts the fold-up crate and the paperwork to the presentation room, where Sally Renshaw sits waiting for us.

When she spies little Tapas, she clutches her chest. "Oh my goodness. He's adorable."

Sally will probably fall madly in love with Tapas and be a foster fail. It's not the worst thing in the world, and I fell victim to the same trap when I fostered Dolly Pawdon. One look at her, and I was smitten.

I hand Tapas's shivering, wiggly body over to Sally, and he gives her a sloppy kiss on her chin. Yep, she's going to be a goner by the end of the foster period.

Hazel slides the paperwork to Sally. "Have you had a chance to review all the information I sent you?"

"Yes. I promise not to take him to dog parks until he's cleared. I'll call you as soon as possible if he doesn't eat or drink."

Hazel nods. "But he may not for the first day because of nerves. Just give him lots of praise and patience, and he'll do fine."

I pull out the supplies from the bag. "We've stocked you with food, a bed, bowls, pee-pee pads, and blankets. If you need anything, just give us a call. And if you have to leave him unattended, please use the crate for his safety... and your furniture's."

As we place the supplies back in the bag, I squeeze the squeaky pig, and Tapas perks up. "He likes this toy."

"Good to know." Sally gives Tapas a scratch under his chin.

While Hazel folds out the crate and secures it in Sally's car, I deposit the supplies in her trunk. Tapas clings to Sally like his life depends on it, but his four pounds is no match for his new foster mom, and she plops him down inside the blanket-filled crate. She frowns as she reaches to pick him up again.

I stop her from snatching Tapas out of the crate. "It's not a punishment. Remember that. He will learn to see it as his little den, and it will help you house-train him."

Sally places the squeaky toy in the crate with Tapas, and he seems entertained enough to forget he's not being held prisoner. "I'll call you tomorrow to let you know how he's doing."

As she drives away, I smile. I walk back inside the animal shelter with a little spring in my step. Happy tears form in my eyes. "I bet Tapas and Sally are going to do well together."

Hazel pats my back. "I hope so because he's too cute for words."

My stomach growls. "Our next appointment isn't until two o'clock. Do you want to grab some lunch?"

She pulls out her phone, scans something, and nods. "Yep, and I have just the place. Want to go with me to Jay's food truck? They're in the park today."

Food truck cuisine doesn't sound very appealing, ever. "I think I'll just get something out of the vending machine." At least junk food has enough preservatives to not give me food poisoning. No telling how many health code violations are swarming around in a restaurant on wheels.

Hazel drags me by the arm from the shelter. "Come on. I heard your stomach. You need some stick-to-your-ribs food. PB&J has a lot to choose from."

I quirk an eyebrow. "And you think food surrounded by diesel fuel is going to do that for me?"

She shakes her head. "Trust me. They have some great stuff on the menu."

I point at her and laugh. "You'd say that if he served cheese and crackers."

Hazel bumps my shoulder with hers. "Guilty, but it's such a nice day to get out for lunch."

That part is true. So far today, we partnered twenty Chihuahuas from a hoarding situation into foster homes, and Tapas was the last to leave. If I'm being completely truthful, I am exhausted and hungry. Even food truck food sounds appetizing.

"Okay. Let's wash the puppy grime off our hands and walk over."

She bounces up and down on her toes. "Yay. And Jay will be excited to see you again. Ever since you worked your magic on Matthew, he considers you an adopted member of the family."

"I enjoyed working with him. It helps when the entire family is on board with my system."

"Let's go."

"After you."

She does a happy dance through the parking lot as my stomach lets out a Great Dane–sized growl.

Hazel rushes up to Jay as he hangs out the window of the brightly colored food truck located on the edge of the park. His baby face lights up when he sees her running toward him. The truck is bright green with PB&J in huge letters surrounded by musical notes that cover the side of the vehicle. It looks like it's seen better days. The smell of hot grease wafts through the air as people line up in front of the window while others mill around, eating their lunches.

Jay waves to me as he hands Hazel two menus, which is really sweet that he remembers me. We only met a few times while I was working with his cousin, but the whole family has been very kind to me, especially now that Matthew is getting married soon. They even invited me to the wedding.

While Hazel finishes her conversation with Jay, I notice another guy handing out food at the back of the truck. His shaggy, dark hair is pulled back in a ponytail, and he wears a baseball cap turned backward. I roll my eyes when he sizes up the girl waiting for her order. *Ugh.* It's like he's imagining her without any clothes on. Total player, and by the smile on his face, he loves every minute of it. In my line of business, he would be classified as a yard dog—perhaps a purebred, but still one hundred percent dog. He's practically slobbering all over himself as he talks to three girls in line now. It's disgusting.

"I got you a menu so you'll know what you want before we get to the window."

As I scan the menu, I frown. "No PB&J? I mean, wouldn't that be funny to have on the menu?"

She grins. "It's a play on words."

"I remember Jay mentioning it. I assume J is for Jay, but that's all I got."

Hazel points to her fiancé. "Well, his name is Jay, but of course, you know that part already." She points to the hot man whore. "And his name is Phin Baxtor. His initials are PB."

"Ah. Clever." I review the menu and release a chuckle. "I think I'll keep it simple and get the Beef Cake burger and Pardon My French fries."

"I always get the BLT. It stands for, Bacon, Lots of bacon, and Top it off with more bacon. It's delicious."

"I think my arteries clogged up just hearing you say that."

When it's our turn at the window, Jay says, "Hey, gorgeous. What will it be today?"

Hazel giggles. "The usual."

Jay pries his gaze from Hazel and turns his attention to me. "Hey there, Amelia. Fancy seeing you here."

"She convinced me." I motion with my head toward Hazel.

"What can I get you?"

I give him my order, then Hazel says, "If you can stump Jay with some music trivia, your meal is on the house."

"And I'm almost never stumped." Jay beams at Hazel. "That one time was an exception, and they'll never find his body." He chuckles at his nonfunny joke.

Challenge accepted. I only have two superpowers, and music trivia is one of them. Since I grew up with my brother and his constant ramblings about his favorite bands, meaningless little factoids are permanently seared into my brain. Other than the fact that I am a beast with cards, useless music trivia is about the only skill I own.

"Okay. Where were the Allman Brothers from?"

Jay scoffs. "Girl. Think of something hard next time. Macon, Georgia."

With a big grin, I shake my head. "Nope."

Over his shoulder, he yells, "Hey, PB, we have someone here who thinks they've stumped me!"

The other guy stops preparing a sandwich, wipes his hands on a towel, and strides over to the front window. He stands tall and stares down at me. The expression on his face makes me feel like he's now imagining *me* naked.

Jay repeats my trivia question, and PB rolls his eyes. "It's Macon."

"Nope." I scroll through my phone until I get to the Allman Brothers website and shove my phone in PB's face.

His cheesy grin fades. "That's…"

"Yep. It says Nashville, doesn't it?"

His eyebrows form a V. "You asked where they were from. It's Macon."

I plant my hands on my hips. "They grew up in Macon but were *from* Nashville. I'd like to add cheese to my free order, please."

I am pretty sure it's the way I bat my eyelashes that really gets his goat. PB scowls at me. "Harrumph."

"All right. If you think I wasn't playing fair, ask me something." I tap my shoe like I'm impatiently waiting.

He holds up a finger. "Wait right there." He leaves the truck window, and after a few seconds, he stomps around from the back of the truck to stand right in front of me. With his arms crossed over his chest, his biceps bulge. "Okay, since you insist." He gets a twinkle in his eyes. "What band features Brian May on guitar?"

Without even having to think hard, I reply, "Queen." I take a step closer to him, so close that I can see the sweat on his brow. "What band's original name was Roundabout?"

His eyes sear into mine. "Deep Purple. Is that all you got?"

We are now so close I need to crane my neck to keep eye contact. "What band got its name from a book by William Henry Davies?"

His mouth opens and closes, like a fish out of water. He peers over at Jay leaning out of the truck, who shrugs.

Boom! I win again.

Jay yells, "PB, get back in here! Orders are piling up."

PB doesn't move. His breaths are shallow as his gaze bores into my eyes.

Hazel places a hand on my shoulders. "Okay, that was enough foreplay for one day."

I gasp, and PB throws his head back with a loud laugh.

While Hazel leads me away, I toss one more barb at PB. "It was Supertramp, by the way."

PB walks backward as a husky chuckle rumbles out of his throat. "Please don't come back, you... trivia rascal."

The customers behind me erupt into cheers. I turn around and bow then, at a snail's pace, slide my debit card back into my wallet and kiss it.

"How did you do that?" Hazel asks.

"It's a gift," I say as I wait for my order.

When the grumpy bear, PB, finishes my order, he shoves it toward me.

"Can I have ketchup with my fries?"

PB points to the bucket of condiment packets. "Over there."

He doesn't let go of my order, and I tug on it.

After I retract it from his grip, I say to Hazel, "I think I like this place. I have tons more trivia, so I could quite possibly eat free for a year."

PB laughs under his breath, and the sultry sound resonates in my bones. He points to Hazel. "I should have known you were friends with *her*. First, you sabotage Jay's bachelorhood, and now, you bring this, this... trivia queen to my truck." He tsks. "You should be ashamed of yourself, Haze."

Hazel takes her order from him and winks. "Aw, PB. No hard feelings, right?"

"Yeah." My grin grows large enough to show my molars. "No hard feelings. Right?"

PB grunts as he focuses on the next order.

While we walk away to find a vacant park bench, I say, "That was fun."

"He still acts like he's mad at me for turning Jay into a romantic sap, but I think he's a little jealous. Phin is actually a really good person once you get through his tough-guy façade." She takes a bite of her BLT, and if it tastes half as good as it smells, it's worthy of the moan she lets out.

I look toward the truck to find PB wiping down the window, and when our eyes meet, he snarls. I can't help but wave. He snatches an order slip off the wire above his head.

"He's cute, isn't he?" Hazel waggles her eyebrows, making me laugh.

"Too cute, and I'm quite sure he knows that already."

Not wanting to talk or even think about PB anymore, I bury my face in the best burger I have ever eaten. The last thing I need is to get the warm fuzzies about a guy. I have more important things to think about, like finding my next client soon. Otherwise, I'll never pay off my debts.

CHAPTER FOUR

Phin

My head is about to explode over that spunky woman who bested me. It was a trick question, but I should have known the answer anyway. The way she sparred with me was both infuriating and attractive.

Nope. Just infuriating.

I was distracted by her cute smile showing that slightly crooked canine tooth, and it caught me off guard. And speaking of canines, from all the dog hair on her T-shirt, which reads "Be the person your dog thinks you are," it looks like she sleeps with a few of them. Just thinking about it makes me want to sneeze.

I hate to give away food, and I certainly hate getting beat at my specialty. But worse than that, it gets my goat that I can't stop staring at her. The way her hair flows around her like she doesn't have a care in the world and how her face glows with sheer beauty without a touch of makeup to cover her cute freckles just does me in. And don't get me started on that simple twang in her voice. She's the real deal, not some transplant wearing cowboy boots and a hat, pretending to be from Nashville. I can smell them a mile away. They're fun to look at, but I know the next stop on their tour list is to get on one of those woo-hoo wagons. Those pedal taverns are the worst modern invention ever. I bet the trivia winner has never stepped foot on one of those things, and I could put money on it that she has never screamed "woo-hoo" going down Second Avenue.

Jay chuckles under his breath, and I give him the death stare. "What?"

He shrugs. "She beat us."

I huff. "Don't remind me."

"And she's cute."

"Aren't they all?" As I clean my workstation, Hazel and the trivia queen walk away to settle down on a park bench and eat their food. I hope that woman likes her freebie because it won't happen again. Ever. If I have to stay up all night learning obscure music trivia, I will. This was just a fluke.

Keep telling yourself that. She knows as much as you, and that pisses you off.

She turns her head my way, and when we lock eyes, a smirk slides across her face. I dip my head, pretending to focus on restocking the napkin holder while I steam. It's one thing to get beat, but it's another to act like a third grader over it.

Jay stashes the cash in a bank bag. "Her name is Amelia."

"Who?"

He snorts. "You know who."

Jay thinks he's slick, but I'm on to his interloping ways. "Don't go there, bro. I can find my own dates."

Jay locks the bank bag inside a briefcase and heads for the back door of the truck. "She's a coworker of Hazel's."

I take a long swig from my water bottle, letting the cool liquid trickle down my throat, wishing it was something stronger.

"And..." He motions in their direction. "She is completely responsible for turning my cousin into marriage material."

I spit out the water, some of the droplets landing on Jay's shirt. "Matthew used to *date* her?"

He stares at the ceiling and lets out a deep sigh. "I swear, I could have said you were the new owner of Beatrice, and you wouldn't have heard me."

I point my water bottle at him. "Oh, I'd hear that."

Jay huffs as he picks up the briefcase. "I'm going to the bank. Amelia was his foster wife, you doofus. Think of it as a trial marriage without the sex."

My face scrunches like I swallowed a lemon. "What's the point of that?"

With a slow shake of his head, he says, "You have a lot to learn, buddy. I think I'm going to refer you to her. She's a miracle worker."

In the distance, I see Hazel and her friend talking as they sit on a nearby park bench. The friend, Amelia, throws her head back and laughs at something Hazel says. "Do you think I need a miracle?"

"You're on this never-ending cycle—smile, date, hook up, see ya later, rinse, repeat."

"And your point is?"

"I don't know what you're so afraid of."

I snatch the briefcase out of Jay's hand. "I'm not afraid of anything. I just know how the relationships will end, so I save myself the pain ahead of time." Plus, Baxtor men don't carry the stick-with-me gene.

Jay scratches his head. "You could break the cycle if you want. Grow a pair."

Clutching my chest with my hands, my jaw drops. "You are worse than my mother. She wants grandbabies so bad that it wouldn't surprise me if she's already ordered a crib."

He shrugs. "Who could blame her?"

I poke him in the chest. "Do not ever say the B word in front of Vivian Baxtor. Ever. Can't we talk about something pleasant, like music?"

Jay looks off toward Hazel. "Music, love... same thing."

A slow shiver runs up my spine. He's so lovey-dovey sometimes that I'm afraid I'll get a cavity from being around him.

"What have you got to lose?" His eyes brighten. "In fact, this could be the perfect way to show the world you're meant to be a bachelor for the rest of your life. What do you say?"

"Why do you care?"

He scans the food truck then grins hugely. "I'll tell you what. We'll bet on it. I am so confident you'll be transformed that I am willing to bet my Beatrice over it."

My head snaps back. I must be in some truck-fume-induced haze, because he couldn't have said what I thought I heard. "You can't be serious. Your Strat? The same one that you won't even let me touch?"

"Yep."

I chew the inside of my mouth, thinking this over. "If I fail the program, I get the Strat."

He nods. "That's how confident I am that you will make it through all the steps. Matthew swears by them."

I place the briefcase down and cross my arms over my chest. "What if I come out of the program being as disgustingly neutered as you?"

Jay grins broadly. "Then, I get the business one hundred percent."

PB&J has been a partnership between us since we started several years ago, when my long-lost father cashed in his chips and bequeathed it to me. Jay and I split the cost and the profits right down the middle, but the truck is mine. This business model has worked well so far, and I didn't even know he wanted more.

"You want my father's truck?"

"It's your truck, but yeah."

"The only thing my father ever gave me. Why would you take that from me, even if I thought you could win it in the first place?"

Jay glances around the beat-up truck. "I think bad mojo here makes you act like your father. You're going to fly through the steps. I get to keep my Strat, and I'll be the sole owner of this fine business."

I hold up a finger. "Wait a second. You keep saying 'steps.' What does that even mean?"

"Amelia will explain."

"Back to the business, what will I do for a job? I mean, I'm not in danger of losing it to you anyway, but I would like to... never mind. Not necessary."

He shrugs. "You can work for me. Or start that catering business you've mentioned."

That is something I've thought of doing to expand the business. Mom would love it if I let the food truck die an ugly death because every time she steps into it, she has flashbacks about the man who abandoned us. Truth be told, from the way she stares at the storage closet, I fear I might have been conceived in there.

I cut my eyes toward Hazel and Amelia as they toss their wrappers in the trash can and walk away. Amelia seems like a pushover. I bet I can make her life so miserable she'll beg me to bug out of the agreement, and I want that Strat so bad I would be willing to deal with an unbearable woman for a few weeks. Plus, she's very easy on the eyes, so it could be fun.

What do I have to lose? My truck, that's what!

"I think I'll take you up on that bet." We shake hands, and I add, "You better sleep with Beatrice while you can because she's going to be mine soon enough."

"You act pretty confident that you can't be changed."

A familiar horn honks, and we turn to see my mom exiting her Mercedes EQA. She waves as she walks in our direction, her hair blowing across her face. We're two peas in a pod, and people say I look just like her. I don't see it, but I definitely get my curly hair from her.

I snatch the briefcase, flip my baseball cap around to its correct position, and puff out my chest. "If I know one thing for sure, it's that I understand women, and none of them has ever bested me. Not one female has been able to change me or crack into this safe I call a brain. It's not possible."

Jay takes out his phone, and his fingers fly over the screen. He then grins. "I'll remind you that you said that."

As Mom approaches us, I mumble, "Do me a favor, and keep her out of the loop about this little bet. I don't need to be double-teamed. Okay?"

"Sure thing." He coughs then mumbles, "Mama's boy."

Jerk.

"Hey, boys. How's business today?" Mom usually stops by this time of day to do a bank run for us. Ever since I got the food truck stuck in the First National Bank drive-through, we all decided it was best that she handle the deposits. And on occasion, she helps us out when we know we'll be swamped with customers. Not to mention her pies are to die for.

I hand Mom the bag. "Nothing out of the ordinary. Business was decent today."

Jay snorts, and Mom scrunches her brows. "Are y'all okay?"

I give Jay the evil eye, so he clears his throat and replies, "Yes, ma'am. See you tomorrow?"

Mom stares at me before she walks backward. "Love you, Phin."

I wave at her retreating frame then smack Jay on the back of the head.

"Ow. Last chance to back out. Are you sure about the bet?"

"Absolutely."

No way will any woman convert me into husband material. It's not possible. But just in case, I'll make sure I'm the worst bachelor on the planet. She'll be in tears by the end of one week. I'm not normally a horrible person, but if I have to be one to get the guitar of my dreams and keep my business, I can be a total jerk for a little while. Amelia won't know what hit her. Even if she is adorable and I felt a slight attraction toward her, especially after she beat me at my trivia game, she is not going to succeed this time. Amelia is about to meet the client of her worst nightmares.

Beatrice, come to Daddy.

CHAPTER FIVE
Amelia

Although I was hesitant to eat at a food truck, my meal was actually one of the best I've had in a very long time. And the fact that I got it for free was icing on the cake. I'll have to get Axel to supply me with a few more mindless bits of information. I never thought my brother's constant jabbering about musical factoids would pay off with a free meal. He'll probably want to eat there, too, especially since he could eat for free daily.

"So, lunch was fun, right?" Hazel types on her phone as we walk back to the animal shelter.

"If you like food truck meals combined with exhaust and a hefty dose of male ego, then I guess it's the perfect place."

She stares a hole through me. "Oh please. You loved it. And I saw how you couldn't keep your eyes off Phin. He's scorching hot, and I know you noticed."

"Did not." *I did, but I won't tell her that.*

"Ha! You guys were throwing out some serious pheromones with all that music trivia bantering. The heat was palpable."

"What? No. That's not what was going on back there." Heat flames my face, and I'm sure my throat is all blotchy with embarrassment.

Hazel's eyes are tiny slits as she watches me squirm. "Suuure." She wiggles her fingers in front of my face, and I bat her hand away. "You scrunch your nose when you're trying *not* to be interested in a guy."

Not wanting to admit that she is right about him being well off the hot-o-meter, I pivot. "He's such a player. I can tell by the way he hit on three women in line in a matter of minutes. That's icky."

"He does have a reputation, but man oh man, he would be a catch if someone had a certain business that could, you know... reform someone like that." She motions to me like she's a model on a game show.

I throw my head back and laugh. "Oh no. He's beyond repair. I take on clients that are difficult but not impossible. That man is way past impossible. Besides, I think he likes how he is, and my clients have to want to change."

She reads something on her phone, and her eyebrow quirks up. "Oh, I don't know about that." She turns her phone so I can read the text message.

Phin wants to hire Amelia as his foster wife.

My eyes grow big. "While I need the work, I don't think I could transform him. And I have a return policy if I cannot revamp my client. I can't afford to spend that much time knowing good and well it's going to be wasted."

Hazel's jaw drops open. "I have never heard you determine someone is beyond repair after one brief encounter. Give him a chance."

"He's just like Bennet but without the hoity-toity stuff."

Hazel rolls her eyes as we enter the shelter to the sound of barking dogs. "From what you've told me about some of your clients, they were as bad if not worse."

The office miniature dachshund wheels toward me, his useless back legs supported by his cart.

I scratch Rosco's chin. "Some were pretty bad, but they wanted to change. This guy... I don't think so. He's a flirt, and that... banter was probably a way to get bigger tips. Didn't work on me. Ha!" I punch my hand in the air victoriously.

"I'll email you his contact info. Just talk to him to see if it's plausible."

I sigh. "If it will make you happy, I'll think about it." Not really, but if it will stop her from pushing this man-bun-wearing, cocky-attitude, as-smooth-as-warm-chocolate dude on me, then I'll pretend to take him seriously.

Hazel organizes supplies for our next foster that will be assigned to a home this afternoon while I stack small cans of wet dog food on the shelf. The pup is a cute little Chinese crested with a skin condition, but he'll be ready for adoption in no time.

"Don't you ever foster a man and think he'd be perfect for you?"

Her words take me by surprise, and my hand sends a column of round dog-food cans sliding off the shelf onto the floor. While I pick up the mess I made, I try to calm my breathing. There might have been a time or two when I started to have feelings for a client.

Jonathan was the closest I came to getting too attached to a client, but we both kept it professional. Even though I think my clients are ready for marriage when I'm finished with them, I can't risk getting hurt by letting them get too personal. Witnessing happiness from afar is way more fulfilling. I tell myself that every day. One day, I might even believe it.

"Nope, and that's not the point. I'm not trying out men for myself under the guise of finding one for someone else."

She dumps a blanket and two squeaky toys into the bag. "Really? You're so sweet. You'd be a great catch for any one of the guys you help." She lets out an adorable sigh as she adopts a starry-eyed expression.

"I want what I have." I sort out all the paperwork and organize the folder for Mrs. Crieve, who will be here in thirty minutes. "I've had multiple chances at true love, and while I'm sorry they didn't work out, I learned from them—not for myself but for others. It makes me happy to make others happy."

"Bennet is an idiot. If I had known you then, I would have knocked some sense into you."

I can always count on Hazel to cut right to the core of the matter. "Yes, but his unwillingness to commit saved me from a lifetime of sadness, even though I also have a massive amount of debt. If he'd had a professional like me to help him a long time ago, it might have turned out differently." I shake the thoughts of Bennet out of my head. He wasn't the one for me, and after I cried my eyes dry, I realized he wasn't worth it. He was my inspiration for my side business, so it wasn't for nothing. "But he's happier being single, and I learned from his behaviors, so I should really thank him."

"Ha. Thank him for dumping you at the altar? You are a much better person than I am. I would have gone all bridezilla on him."

Grabbing the folder and the bag of supplies, I take them to the meet-and-greet room to prepare for Mrs. Crieve. "It's all good. I have no hard feelings, and I love helping people get ready to fall in love. It's very rewarding work. Just like getting these adorable critters ready for their *furever* homes."

My phone beeps, and I see a text from a number I don't recognize.

It reads, *I understand you can turn off my womanizing ways.*

Ugh.

Hazel giggles. "Is that from Phin?"

"I assume so."

I text him back, *See attached documents for you to review. I want you to be aware of the agreement. If you cannot commit wholeheartedly, I won't waste my time.*

That ought to scare him off, and to remind him of who he's dealing with, I add *Supertramp* to the salutation on the message.

Trying to watch *The Bachelor* with my nephew climbing all over me is nearly impossible. I love him like crazy, but he and peanut butter do not make for a clean experience.

"Want some?" He shoves the slobbery, half-eaten sandwich in my face.

"No, thank you, but that was very sweet of you to offer."

He drops the sandwich in my lap, sneezes in my face, then climbs off the couch, almost crushing Dolly Pawdon in the process. She lets out a yip before she runs away to my room, which is where I should go.

"Did he choose 'the one' yet?" Dorothy scoops up the sandwich and takes a bite.

Blech. She never used to do things like that before she had kids. She hands the sandwich to her husband, Dax, and he also eats a bite.

Through a mouthful of peanut butter, Dax says, "Not yet. He's narrowed it down to three. I'm really hoping Luke picks Francessa. She didn't freak out when a bee was buzzing around her during the picnic scene."

It's humorous how committed he is to the show, even though he regularly denies watching it.

Dorothy props her feet on the coffee table. "I bet you anything her name is really Francine."

I giggle, thinking she's probably right, but Francessa makes for better ratings.

Dax shakes his head. "It's really Francessa. I googled it."

Dorothy and I stare at him, taking in his confession.

When he notices us, he asks, "What?" He swallows the bite of sandwich and asks me, "Any leads on new clients?"

Nice change of subject, dude.

I'm not sure if he's asking because he's curious or if he's tired of me freeloading. It's only been a few days, far less than my usual dry spell between clients. "Maybe, but I don't know if he meets my eligibility criteria."

"How's that?" Dorothy finishes off Tucker's sandwich.

"Because he's a man—"

Dorothy raises her eyebrows, and I stop from saying a not-so-nice word around her three-year-old. Dax is at the ready to cover his son's ears if necessary.

"I get the impression he likes the way he is, so I'm not sure why he would want to reach out to me in the first place."

Tucker digs in his nose and pulls out the mother lode of a booger then wipes it on his shirt.

Dorothy laughs as she hands Tucker a tissue. "Maybe I should do a foster-motherhood program."

I point a finger at her. "That's not a bad idea."

"I was kidding."

Dax shakes his head. "No way. People might find out we're just winging it like everyone else."

"True." Dorothy and Dax knuckle bump.

"I sent Phin the documents anyway. He's supposed to get back to me if he's still interested, which means I will probably never hear from him again. And that's fine with me."

Dorothy gets all dreamylike. "Phin. Yum. That name oozes charisma."

Dax quirks an eyebrow, so Dorothy kisses him on the cheek. "Not as much as yours does, sweetie."

I roll my eyes then say to Dax, "You should see him in action. He's a ladies' man if there ever was one."

Tucker hands me the booger-filled tissue. "What's a ladies' man?"

Dax doubles over laughing and, in return, gets smacked in the side by his wife.

Dorothy cocks her head to the side. "Yeah, Aunt Amelia. What's a lady's man?"

I clear my throat. "Well... that's when a man does things to make ladies notice him."

Tucker looks up at his mom. "I'm a lady's man."

Dorothy tickles her little man, and I let out a chuckle. "You stick to being cute for now."

My phone chimes, and I excuse myself to my room to read the email. It's from Phin, saying he's read the documents and doesn't have any questions. He wants to know when we start. No way did he read everything I sent him, because he would have had at least one question. They always have questions.

I settle down into my bed and close my eyes. The only thing worse than not having a client is having one that's not going to take it seriously.

A bang on my door jolts me out of my thoughts. "Auntie Amelia, can you wipe my butt?"

I don't know why Tucker sought me out to do the honors when he has two perfectly capable parents in the living room. I scrub my face and decide, no matter how difficult this client might be, I need out of Dorothy's house as soon as possible.

My phone chirps with an incoming text. Jeez, this guy is persistent. His text reads, *Well?*

My phone chirps, announcing an email. I let out a groan when I see it's from one of my credit card companies. I got one company off my back with what Jonathan owed me, but that didn't make a dent in the balance. And this one has been hounding me for a month. In hindsight, I should have given both cards a tiny payment just to stave off the debt collectors, but I wasn't thinking. Now if I don't give them the minimum balance due, which I can't even afford, I will be turned over to a collection agency. I need to do whatever it takes to get out from under this expense I created to keep up with Bennet's lifestyle. I have to remember to deposit the cash tip Jonathan gave me tomorrow. That should keep them off my back a bit longer.

I send Phin a text before I talk myself out of it. *How about we meet at five o'clock tomorrow in the park?*

He sends me a thumbs-up emoji. For the first time since I started this business, I have my doubts about my ability to modify a guy's thought process. If I can reform Phin, I can fix anyone, but I need his money, and the clock is ticking.

CHAPTER SIX
Phin

While I sit on a park bench, waiting for Amelia to show up, I flip through the printouts from her email. Not that I read everything, but I get the gist of it. She mother-hens me to death until I bow down and pretend that I'm a new man. Easy peasy. With a little bit of acting, I could get rid of her in a week. And I'll be the new proud owner of that beautiful Stratocaster. This is going to be like taking candy from a baby.

I notice her from across the trail. She stops at every dog and pets its head like a real live version of Snow White. All that's missing is for her to break out into song. As if she can read my mind, she catches my eye and smiles. After one more pat to the head of a golden retriever, she jogs toward me. When she gets close, I read her shirt. It says, "It wasn't me. It was the dog." I stand and offer a hand to shake.

"You must be Amelia, the trivia queen."

She lets out a breathy chuckle as she shakes my hand with a grip that could cripple an arm wrestler. "Yes, it helps to have a musician in the family."

At least she has one redeeming quality.

She takes a deep breath and becomes all businesslike. "Thanks for meeting me. It's best to make sure we are on the same page before you sign the paperwork and send your deposit."

Dumbfounded, I ask, "Deposit?"

Amelia sits on the park bench and pulls the paperwork from her bag that's almost as big as she is. "I don't work for free. My service comes complete with a money-back guarantee, so if I determine you've put in the time and effort and you aren't fully satisfied, you get a re-fund."

"How much?"

She cocks her head. "It was stated in the contract I emailed you."

"Yeah, but—"

Amelia huffs and organizes the documents then puts them back in her bag. "I only work with clients who are serious about reforming. If you aren't going to take the initiative to do the simple things like read-ing the procedure manual, how can I trust you will be serious about the steps?"

"Ah yes, the steps." I add a knowing nod in hopes she believes I've read it all.

An ice-cold stare beams onto my head, and I need to back up and start over. Okay, maybe this will take a little longer than a week. Ten days tops. "I mean, I *will* read the information. I promise. Could you just give me the abbreviated version?"

"It's apparent you will need to be on the leash for much longer than my usual clients."

I belt out a laugh. "I don't do bondage."

Amelia gasps and stands. "Good day, Mr. Phin Baxtor."

Goodbye, Beatrice. She stomps away, taking any hopes of me win-ning the bet with her. It can't be over this soon. I rush toward her and latch onto her arm. "Wait. I'm sorry. Let's start over. Just explain your system in simple terms. You have to agree, telling a grown man he'll be put on a leash does tend to bring out kinky thoughts."

Amelia yanks out of my grasp and puts her hands on her hips. "I take this job seriously, and if you can't do the same, then I need to seek another client. You are not the only dog in the kennel, you know."

Dog in the kennel?

Rushing around to block her retreat, I realize how cute she is in a nonflashy, take-me-as-I-am kind of way. She smells like a freshly baked cinnamon roll. "I'm sorry. I talk too much sometimes."

She snorts and stares up at me for the longest time as she taps her foot. Right when I think she's going to bolt, she pulls out the paperwork and a pen. "Fine. If you really want to do this, just sign the contract, and we can start fresh tomorrow when I move in."

The pen rolls out of my hand and onto the grass. "You... move in with me?"

Through gritted teeth, she adds, "Yes. I can only train you properly if we spend all our waking moments together. And based on the background check I did last night, you pass the test."

My eyes grow wide. "You did *what*?"

Her eyes narrow. "Section three, paragraph two states that I do not work with clients with even the slightest record. One parking ticket, neighbor dispute, noise ordinance complaint, anything, and I remove myself from the agreement."

"Wow. That's cold."

"A girl has to know who she's dealing with." She holds the papers under my nose. "Just sign, please. As soon as the deposit is in my Venmo account, we will begin the process."

Beatrice. Beatrice. Beatrice.

I sign on the dotted line. "Just curious, how long does this process usually take?"

She shrugs as she signs the form. "It really depends. For a man who is resistant to the process, it could take much longer than usual. Two or three months. Maybe longer."

What the...?

I swallow the words I want to spill and grind out, "That sounds... lovely."

She points to my phone. "You might want to send me the deposit now so we can proceed."

"Yes. The deposit. It's, uh..."

With a deadpan voice, she says, "Five thousand dollars. Like the contract states."

"Five thousand dollars?" I screech.

Amelia takes the paperwork and holds it sideways as if she's about to rip it to shreds.

I stop her and add, "Wait. Here ya go."

I punch my phone so hard transferring the deposit into her account that I think I might break the glass. "Here. Is. Your. Money."

Her phone chimes, and she inspects her message. When her grin grows wide, she reaches out to shake my hand again. "Okay. I will make copies of the contract, and don't worry. Your money will be safely placed in a non-interest-bearing account until our business is done. What time in the morning is good for you?"

"My day starts really early, so how about six o'clock?"

She blinks those big brown eyes and takes a step backward.

"If that's too early, maybe this arrangement won't work for *you*." I feel a small but significant victory coming.

"Nope. It's fine. I'll get used to it. I'm assuming you have an extra bedroom for me to live in during the process."

Unfortunately, I do. It's full of supplies for my food truck, including a massive extra refrigerator that hums so loud I can hear it from outside my apartment. But she doesn't have to know that just yet. "Of course."

"Jingle me your address, and I'll see you bright and early tomorrow."

Jingle? Dear Lord, I am *dealing with Snow White.* "You bet."

"Toodles." She prances off, her ponytail whipping around her face and with five thousand dollars of my money in her account. When I get my hands on Jay, I'm going to give him a piece of my mind. But I can't. He needs to think I'm cool with this. If I back out now, I'll never get that guitar.

I pull out my phone and call Jay. When he answers, I say, "You get your cousin on the phone. Five thousand dollars?"

He chuckles so much that if he were in front of me instead of on the phone, I would punch him. "Ah, I guess you met with Amelia. But, bro, it's all worth it. You'll see. I'm texting him right now."

"Ask him what leash training is."

He belts out a huge laugh. "Buddy, I'll give you a hint. In her mind, you are a dog, and she'll treat you like that until you are ready to be adopted."

I scrunch my brow. "What are you talking about?"

"She's a foster coordinator at the animal shelter, and she uses the same techniques on men."

"That's the stupidest thing I've ever heard."

"Don't knock it. It works. Have fun, bro. Matthew says to stay away from the fleas and have fun during playtime."

He disconnects the call before I can ask what the heck he's talking about. Perhaps I should have read the manual.

CHAPTER SEVEN
Amelia

Dorothy gives me another hug as I drag my belongings to my beat-up Ford Focus—all I could afford after my Lexus was repossessed. She hands me Dolly's carrier, and with a single paw sticking out, it's like Dolly is waving goodbye.

I drive the short distance to Phin's apartment. I still cannot believe I agreed to foster him. He's clearly not husband material, but I really need the money. If I can reform him, I can handle *any* man.

I drive up to the Clairmont apartment complex and let out another big yawn. Barely getting my car in park, I see Phin wheeling huge bins down the sidewalk toward his food truck, which is parked at the edge of the parking lot. His biceps bulge against his PB&J T-shirt as he places the bin next to the tire, and I'm beginning to think that baseball cap is glued to his head. That's a shame because he should let those curls flow. Maybe it's a health department code or something.

He didn't exaggerate when he said he gets started early. On his way back up the sidewalk, he pauses. His eyes get big, and he stalks over to my car like I'm his prey.

"Hello... wife."

I curtsy. "Are you double-dog sure you want to do this?"

He clenches his fist then releases to shake out his hands. After a deep breath, Phin nods.

"What do you prefer to be called? PB, Phin, Mr. Baxtor?"

"Phin is fine."

I grin in hopes we are getting off on the right foot. "Okey dokey, Phin."

He gestures with his arm. "Let me show you my humble abode."

After I retrieve my bag and tri-fold display case from my trunk, I follow him toward apartment number 113. I do my best to keep my eyes off his tight butt, and it's a mighty fine tushy. I give myself a mental slap across the face to remind myself that the only reason I should be checking out a client's physique is if there is any room for improvement. That is definitely not the case with Phin, so my eyes must stay above the shoulders from here on out.

Not watching where I was going, I stub my toe on an uneven section of the sidewalk and stumble into Phin. I latch on to his waist to right myself. "Oops."

He stiffens as he stares at me. "I keep telling my landlord I'm going to break my neck over that one day. Glad it was almost your neck and not mine." He grins then adds, "Just kidding. My place isn't anything special, but the apartment manager lets me park my truck here, so it's worth it. Plus... well, you'll see soon enough."

"You'd be surprised at some of the living situations I've endured."

"With the rate you're charging, I assumed you're used to mansions."

"My client Jonathan had an amazing apartment, but most bachelors would rather spend their money on toys, not on a home. One time, I had to share a room with a python." I shiver at the memory. "One full month without a complete night's sleep. I was always worried I would get squeezed to death. You don't have snakes, do you?"

"No pets at all."

He opens the door for me, and the scent of smoky meat lingers in the air.

The living quarters are sparse, with the standard-issue bachelor couch, lounger, and massive TV for watching sports, no doubt, but most interesting is the large number of guitars hanging on the walls, lining the living room. Acoustic, electric, and even a dobro are all part of his display. Most of my clients have some type of collection, like action figures or golf clubs, so it's no surprise that Phin has an assortment of something.

"Wow."

Phin puffs out his chest. "You like my ax selection?"

"No, your guitars."

"Same thing... never mind."

I walk past them and admire each one. Not that I'm an instrument junkie, but I can easily tell most of these are not starter pieces. "My brother would be slobbering if he saw this."

"The musician in your family? The other trivia expert?"

"Yep. Axel plays the cello in the Nashville Symphony. But he can play at least twelve instruments."

His eyes pop. "Twelve? What kind?"

On my fingers, I count off. "Cello, violin, viola, guitar, bass guitar, drums, mandolin, steel guitar—"

"I get it. He's a prodigy. Can I marry him?"

I bust out laughing. "No bromance with my brother, please. But you will get to meet him during one of our playdates. Actually, it's a good thing you have something in common with one of my siblings. It'll be good practice to see how you mesh with a potential wife's family."

Phin blinks as he cocks his head to the side.

I roll my eyes. "Of course, you skipped that part in the document about the meet and greet. Shocker."

He cringes. "Sorry. I'm more of a big-picture guy. Details like that bore me."

This is such a bad idea. It's obvious he's not committed.

"So, boss, what next?"

Dolly growls, making Phin jump. "Holy crap. What is that?"

I open the pet carrier, and Dolly slinks out, taking in her new surroundings. "Phin, meet Dolly Pawdon. She's a Chihuahua, Italian greyhound, rat terrier mix. Isn't she adorable?"

"More like a rat terror. She looks like a pull-apart dog with her head being one color and legs being all different ones."

"My father says the exact same thing."

He backs away when Dolly sniffs his legs. "You didn't say there would be pets involved."

"Ha. Section three, paragraph four. And it's obvious you have no idea how much pets will be a part of the process."

"I don't like dogs."

I pick up Dolly. "Isn't she cute? She's very sweet, and she'll be good. I promise."

Phin scowls as he scratches the back of his head. "As long as she doesn't leave surprises on the floor and..." He leans down to face Dolly, who kisses him on the nose. "You will never sleep with me. Got it?"

Lick, lick.

Famous last words. All men are pushovers for Dolly. It's only a matter of time. My last client, Jonathan, wasn't a canine lover, either, but one time, I found him out in the rain with an umbrella over Dolly while she found her potty spot. His Armani suit was drenched, but Dolly stayed completely dry. *That* is husband material.

"What if my apartment has a no-pet policy?"

"I already checked and paid the pet fee—or *you* paid the fee."

"What if I'm allergic?"

I walk toward him and stare him down. "You checked 'no' on the application."

He growls, making Dolly cock her head to the side.

"Mr. Baxtor, if you don't like this business arrangement, I can leave right now. I will not be questioned every step of the way." I poke his chest with my finger for added emphasis. "And if you feel the need to get mouthy with me on things that are clearly stated in the document *you* signed, I will break the contract, and you will not have to ever see me again, or your deposit." I scratch behind Dolly's ears. "In fact, I think it's best that I back out of this deal right now before I strangle you." Turning on a dime, I wheel my luggage toward the door, but my display case slips out of my grip and bangs into the wall.

A warm, calloused hand covers mine, and in a soft, kind voice, he says, "I'm sorry. Please, don't leave. I will try to cooperate. I may suck at it, but I will at least try."

I glance down at his hand covering mine and notice the bulging veins of a man who works hard with his hands, both professionally and in his hobby. I slip my hand out of his and walk toward the row of guitars, still holding Dolly. Trying to diffuse the situation, I say, "You do have quite the collection here."

Phin stands next to me and points to a rough-looking acoustic guitar. I don't know much about instruments, but it doesn't look like it's anything valuable, certainly not anything worth displaying. "That was the first guitar I ever owned. I saved my money when I was twelve, and my mother took me down to this used store called Dirt Cheap Music, and I bought it. The owner threw in a few lessons, and I've been hooked ever since."

I glance over my shoulder to see his expression change from cocky know-it-all to nostalgic. I can work with this. *Note to self. When Phin gets defensive, pivot and talk about music.*

"You can't bear the thought of parting with it?"

He shrugs. "Yeah."

"Hmmm. So you *are* capable of forming attachments. Good to know."

Phin throws his head back in a large laugh, and it rumbles through the small apartment. "To things, yes. To people? Not so much. Let's just say you have your work cut out for you."

I throw my shoulders back. "I can handle a challenge as long as you're open-minded. But first things first. Where is my room?"

He gets an evil twinkle in his eyes, making me think I should run for the door. "Right this way, ma'am."

I follow him down a short hallway lined with photos of himself with musicians. They are all autographed to Phin, and even though I can't make out most of the signatures, the artists seem familiar. I'm sure Axel would know every one of them.

"Are these your idols?"

"Definitely." He points to one. "You probably don't know who this is, but he wrote a ton of famous songs. He's so down-to-earth and has inspired me to be focused on writing as well as playing."

"Very cool."

He clears his throat as if he has given too much information into what makes him tick. "Bathroom is on the left. I only have one, so we'll have to share. As you can see, I don't do much primping."

"You just let me know when you need in there, and I'll work around your schedule."

"Harrumph. My room is over there and completely off limits." He stares at Dolly. "Do you understand?"

"Absolutely." I get the feeling he's trying to get a rise out of me, so I won't give him the pleasure.

He opens the door across the hall from his and leans against the doorframe. "This is yours for... as long as you're here."

I cross the threshold and am taken aback by the amount of stuff stored in what would normally be a second bedroom. Shelves filled with food items line one entire wall while another wall is stocked floor to ceiling with plastic bins. In the corner is a massive commercial refrigerator with three glass doors, and I see no bed in sight.

"Uh, where am I supposed to sleep?"

He snaps his fingers. "Oh, I've got you covered." He places my display case against the wall, opens the closet to pull out a box, and hands it to me. "This is for you."

He has to be kidding. "A blow-up mattress?"

"Is that a problem? I bought a good one." He motions toward the floor. "See, you can lay it in the middle of the room at night then lean it up against this wall during the day. Oh, and I cleared out some closet space for your clothes."

Phin motions to the closet to show me a space about a foot wide to store my belongings.

I'm pretty sure I should cut my losses now. I could just send back his deposit and walk away, but I think he wants me to back out of the agreement, so I will do the exact opposite. I examine the box and grin. "Wow. It comes with its own pump too. How very thoughtful of you. Thank you. You're the best."

He backs toward the door. "I'll let you get settled in. I've got to get to work. I left you a key on the kitchen counter. See you this afternoon?"

"Absolutely. I'll explain all the details. That's where this comes in handy." I point to my display case.

"Will there be a test?"

Grinning, I say, "Several."

His shoulders slump. "I was never good at school."

My smile widens. "But this time, you have a personal tutor to help you every step of the way. We will cover all the basics and get started on phase one."

Phin's eyebrows pull together. "What is phase one?"

"Crate training."

With a slow shake of his head, he says, "You are the strangest person I have ever met."

"Guilty. See you later."

He's going to fail before the week is over, but I have to try. Something about him makes me want to reform him, like he has a lot to offer. I think somebody has hurt him so deeply in the past that he thinks he's beyond repair. But that was before I got ahold of him. With my techniques, I can transform this bad boy with a questionable past into a man worthy of settling down.

After giving Dolly a kiss, I open the closet and make room for my sparse belongings. Without meaning to, I tip over a basket of what appears to be business cards in the shape of guitar picks—shocker—that have the PB&J logo on them. Some have crumpled. While I do my best to stack them back into the basket, I notice phone numbers written on them, and a handful also have lipstick prints. Ugh.

I toss the cards back into the basket, pull out the mattress from the box, and start blowing it up. As soon as the pump kicks in, Dolly scurries away from the noise. This is my home for the next several months, so I need to make the most of it. It could be worse. It could smell like fish. While the mattress plumps up and Phin meanders in and out, getting supplies, I jot my first journal entry on my phone. This is going to be the hardest assignment ever.

Phin Baxtor Journal Entry 1

New client referred to me. Reluctant to change.

Background: From what I found online, he does not serial date. It is unclear how intimate he gets with his dates, but if his stack of "calling cards" is any indication, he does not lack offers for a good time. My guess is the crumpled cards are those he has already had his fun with, but not sure why he would feel the need to keep them unless it's to make sure he doesn't accidentally date the same person twice.

It's also worth mentioning he can form attachments to people, as obvious by the framed pictures in the hallway. Even though they are not personal relationships, he has the ability to reach out when it includes something he is interested in. Another item to mention is that he does have the ability to connect with things (guitars) and even keeps the first guitar his mother bought. This shows he is sentimental and holds his mother in high regard.

Music and discussing the topic calms him. It's his happy place. I will add that to my steps. In order to get him ready (and use his money to pay my debts), I need to act fast. My steps may have to be consolidated. As long as he successfully completes the program, I will be one step closer to accomplishing my goal as well.

CHAPTER EIGHT

Phin

The pump's high-pitched whirring puts a grin on my face as I organize the rest of the supplies for today's menus. Amelia places her shoulder as close as possible to one ear as she texts something on her phone. It just occurred to me that I will have to come into this room while she's still sleeping, which will be awkward at best.

I must do stupid crate training or leash or whatever it is at breakneck speed.

I scoot past her to retrieve the burger patties, hot dogs, and the bacon from the refrigerator, making that fleabag of hers perk up. The dog's nose catches a whiff of the meat, and I give her an evil stare and dare her to come near me as I shove them into a cooler to keep them cold.

Amelia turns off the pump, and the silence is deafening. She slides the phone onto the floor and plops down on the mattress, causing her dog to tackle her, covering Amelia's face with sloppy kisses. "It's actually not bad at all. I mean, at first, I thought you were trying to make me miserable, but I might have to buy one of these." She flops around like a bug on its back, making the mattress squish with every move.

I fight to hold in the growl. She wasn't supposed to like it. If she's that easy to please, I'll have to up my game and create the most uncomfortable living situation as possible, which won't be hard. I am a guy, after all. I haven't been roped into marriage or even a long-term commitment for a reason, and I will put my finely honed bachelor skills to good use.

"What will you do with the dog while you're at work? I don't want that thing running around my apartment, sleeping on my couch, tearing up my rugs. Or worse, leaving surprises on the floor."

Amelia rolls off the mattress then stands, dusting the hairs off her shirt, which says, "My dog is my copilot." "Oh, don't worry about that. Dolly comes with me most days. She helps socialize new pups who have been in hoarding or neglectful situations."

"Sounds... so depressing."

"Not at all. I love it."

Of course Mary Poppins would love it. I'm shocked she only has one animal. She looks like the type who would adopt them all and become a crazy cat lady before she's thirty.

"Well, I need to get to work. Gotta feed a lot of hungry city folk today."

"What time will you be home?"

I quirk an eyebrow. "If you must know, my normal routine is to finish the lunch rush around two o'clock then hit the gym, practice my music for a while, then go out."

She does this judgy head-tilt thing. "Out?"

"Yes. Out."

"You can't go out."

"It's Friday. I always go to Hooskers on Friday nights."

An evil grin slides across her face. "Not anymore you don't. Phase one is crate training."

I point my finger at her. "You are one sick, twisted chick."

Her eyes narrow, and I feel suddenly naked. "If you read the contract—"

"Well... I have to get to work." I hitch my thumb over my shoulder as I back toward the door.

"No going out until you are crate trained. I suggest you read the contract. See you tonight at five o'clock sharp. We have lots to go over."

"I'm out of here."

"I'm serious. Tonight, we go over the plan and start with phase one."

I scrub my face with my hands. "You seem like a reasonable person. Can't you just give me an aptitude exam to see if I can be exempt from certain steps? I'm a pretty smart guy."

With a deadpan voice, she replies, "I'm sure you are. I do not have anything like that, and if I did..." She stands and pats my chest patronizingly. "I have a feeling you would fail, miserably."

My eyebrows raise at her bluntness. "Wow. You don't pull any punches."

"Nope."

My hand covers hers as I peel hers away from my chest. "You need to learn the meaning of fun."

Her mouth drops open. "I am so much fun." She gets a twinkle in her eyes. "What band started off playing on the Jersey Shore?"

"Pfft. You are never going to get a free meal with that lame try."

I walk backward out of the room, and when I turn to leave, she says from behind me, "Well?"

"Bruce Springsteen and the E Street Band. Try harder next time."

"Have a nice day." That singsong voice is going to give me a migraine.

"Harrumph."

Driving my food truck white-knuckled the entire time, I hear Amelia's annoying, perky voice in my head. I wonder if she's even perky in her sleep. That kind of constant enthusiasm is exasperating, but then she goes and spouts music trivia like she's reciting the Pledge of Allegiance. At least she has one redeeming quality along with her cuteness. That is definitely *not* annoying. But if she thinks she's going to stick me in a wire cage, she's got another think coming.

I stew all the way to the mall parking lot where we'll set up today. It's quite possible I am going to wear down my molars after this little adventure. In fact, I may have to get dentures after just one morning with that girl. She may love all her dog analogies, but if she's talking about shutting me down and giving me dog treats as compensation, I may have to let go of the dream of owning Beatrice.

Jay is already at the site, waiting for me when I arrive. I slam the truck door loudly, making him jump.

"Crate training? What the heck is that?"

He throws his head back and belts out a laugh. "It's not as bad as it sounds. Matthew swears by it."

"It sounds pretty awful. I can't believe I'm paying for the privilege too."

"It'll be worth every penny."

Beatrice. "Whatever, man. I am not a dog."

"It's just terminology. You'll see." He slides out the canopy, sets up the menu board, and begins to write the specials for today.

His handwriting is way better than mine, so I let him take on that chore. One time, people thought we were selling all-beet patties, and we didn't figure out why no one ordered a burger that day until the end of the lunch period.

"She says I can't go out tonight. Who does she think she is telling a grown man what he can and cannot do?"

Jay plugs in the generator and flips a switch to initiate battery power to the truck. "Something about being able to assimilate back into the world once you learn how to handle being alone first."

I point with a large knife in my hand. "Hey, I know how to be alone. I've practically mastered the art of being alone." A noise in the parking lot alerts me to my mother's arrival. "Can we talk about this later?"

"What's this about my favorite son being alone?" Mom flashes me that smile that can make any rainy day full of sunshine as she approaches the trailer.

"I'm your only son."

She hands me and Jay each a cup of coffee and a bag of what smells like the finest bagels in Nashville. We dive into the bag, knowing we'll need some serious carbs to get through the lunch rush.

I jerk a thumb toward Jay. "Mr. Whipped wants me to get programmed into being someone I'm not."

She hands the bank bag to Jay, and he proceeds to count the money and place it in the cash drawer.

"What does that mean?" Mom fills the napkin holder and proceeds to lay out the customers' supplies.

"It's not for me. I'm not ready for a committed relationship."

Mom sips her coffee and takes in my words. "You never will be at this rate."

My jaw drops. Mom usually has my back, but like most women her age, she longs for grandchildren. The thought of that kind of commitment sends a wave of shivers down my spine.

"I'm doing just fine, thank you very much."

Jay slams the register closed and crosses his arms. "I assume you haven't told her yet."

I think I need a new business partner and a new best friend.

Mom glances from Jay to me and cocks her head. I keep very few things from my mother. For as long as I can remember, it was just her and me against the world. She knows me better than anyone.

I clear my throat. "Mom, Jay convinced me to... hire the girl who got his cousin in tip-top shape to be husband material."

Her eyes widen. "That's amazing. I mean, she won't have to do much except tidy up some of your rough edges—"

"Rough edges? Mom. Harsh." I stomp into the food truck and busy myself with getting items ready for the lunch crowd.

She enters behind me and squeezes my shoulders. "You know what I mean."

Maybe if I ignore her, she'll drop it.

"What's her name?"

I let out a deep, groaning sigh. "Amelia."

"That's a pretty name. Can I meet her?"

Not happening. "Nope."

Jay shakes his head. "Dude, at some point, there's a family event, so... yeah."

Mom does one of those quick cheerleader claps. "I can't wait."

"Don't get your hopes up, Mom. She's a Pollyanna-ish dog lover."

With a dreamy expression, she replies, "Sounds lovely."

I roll my eyes.

"But he has to be crate trained first."

Mom bites her lip then bends over in a fit of giggles. While I stare at her, she swallows her laughter. "I'm sorry, son, but you have to admit..."

"Yeah. Jay says it would make sense if I read the contract."

Jay shrugs as he logs into the iPad. "Crate training means you get comfortable living in your small space, know where to call home, creating a man cave, so to speak."

"I have that already."

Mom shakes her head. "You have a bachelor pad. It's not the same thing."

"Okay, I'll go buy some candles and throw pillows. Would that move me to the next phase?"

Jay snorts. "You're just trying to get Bea—"

I stare at Jay, and he swallows his words. Mom would not like it if she knew I was doing this to win a bet.

"What's that?" Mom asks.

"It's nothing. Jay is just being a jerk. Right now, I have a job to do."

She pinches my cheek. "You know I love you and only want what's best for you."

Like having babies.

Mom squeezes me around the middle. "I can stay for the lunch crowd if you think you'll need it."

I never turn down free help, even if it means the interrogation will continue. "That would be great."

Mom punches her fist in the air. "Yes! And you can tell me all about your new girlfriend."

Jay's laughter is interrupted by my smack to his gut. Tonight is going to be the hardest of all. If I can slip into my room, pull up the sports network, and ignore the cute interloper for eight hours, I'll be golden. Somehow, I have a sinking feeling none of this is going to go my way. I have to up my game to make her miserable and show I am unable to change. That should be easy because I can't.

Mom has extra pep in her step, and I can't help but think she assumes this program will help me, so for her sake, I will put in a tiny bit of effort, then I can honestly tell her I tried. But Mom can't know about the bet. She would be so disappointed in me if she knew, and I never want to hurt my mother.

CHAPTER NINE
Amelia

By the time I finish up for the day and arrive back at Phin's apartment, his food truck is already in the parking lot. The first night is always a bit nerve-racking and can make or break the contract. My go-to first evening usually includes a home-cooked meal and some kind of icebreaker. Jonathan was used to having his meals cooked for him, but he actually relaxed and enjoyed the process. Matthew was a take-out kind of guy, and I don't think he ever got the hang of it completely, but he was able to master a few decent meals with pride. Those clients were willing to put the effort into it, and I hope Phin decides soon to get serious about my system. It's obvious I need to think of creative ways to make the contract work with Phin. My sanity depends on it.

"Come on, Dolly. Let's get this show on the road." I pick up her carrier, and as I approach his door, I notice the groceries I ordered have already arrived and sit next to the front door. The least he could have done was bring the bags inside. For crying out loud, he had to step over them to get inside.

After unlocking the door, I pick up one grocery bag and scoot the other with my foot until I'm inside. I'm taken aback by the pigsty of a mess in the living room. Newspapers and guitar magazines lie all over the floor. Empty beer bottles cover the coffee table as Phin sits in the recliner watching a concert, wearing nothing but his boxer briefs. I can't stop gawking at the mess and the guy relaxing in the chair. He has the perfect muscle-to-frame ratio, and a nice little happy trail of hair peeks out from his waistband. If I weren't fuming, I might see the man before me in a more pleasing manner. But put in context, I'm close to seeing red.

He grins at what I can only imagine is my stunned expression. When we both left for work, the apartment was decently organized and picked up. I never expect men to be clean freaks, but it's apparent he went out of his way to be a slob.

"Welcome home, roomie," he says as he chews on an unlit cigar.

I snatch it out of his mouth and bite my tongue to keep the response I want to give from slipping out of my mouth. Instead, I focus on Dolly. "He's been busy."

With a shy grin, he replies, "Oh, I guess I should have picked up around the place before you got here. Where are my manners?"

I release Dolly from her carrier, and she immediately rushes to Phin, making him crawl into a ball.

"Down, fleabag."

"She's just trying to say hello."

He snaps the recliner to a sitting position, and Dolly takes the opportunity to jump into his lap. She covers him with kisses as he does his best to extricate himself from her and the chair.

"Aw, she likes you."

"Blech." Phin takes the wiggly canine and plants her on the floor as he stands and stretches.

I jut my chin high. "I guess you were too busy picking up the place to read the text message I sent about groceries being delivered."

"Oh... so that's what that was."

"Yeah," I deadpan. "I could see you approved the order, so I charged them to your Venmo account. Whatever spoiled is not out of my pocket."

His face loses that smirk. "You can't do that."

"It's stated in the—"

He holds up a hand to interrupt me. "Yeah, yeah." He motions toward the galley kitchen. "Help yourself."

My sneer over my shoulder pins him in his place. "I am not your cook, and I'm not your maid. Now, go wash your hands, and put on some clothes, then clean up the living room."

Phin cocks his head to the side but doesn't move. I motion with my hand toward his bedroom. "Go."

He groans but walks down the hall. "You're worse than my mother."

"I heard that."

"Yeah, well, it's because I wanted you to." He slams the door as I put the groceries away and realize the delivery person forgot to include chicken, the main item on the menu. It's obvious we aren't cooking tonight.

A few moments later, he returns wearing a clean T-shirt and basketball shorts. "So, Betty Crocker, what are we having for dinner?"

"Aren't you forgetting something?" I gesture toward the living room. "Chop-chop."

I leisurely walk into the room, plop down in his recliner, and slap my thigh to invite Dolly onto my lap. I fwap the foot rest up and exhale loudly. "I'll be right here waiting for you to finish."

"No one sits on my throne," he grinds out, making the muscles in his jaw flex.

"I just did."

His mouth gapes open. "I..." With shoulders slumped, he picks up the magazines and organizes them on the coffee table. "You. Are. Impossible."

"Not really." I point to a magazine peeking out from under the couch. "You missed one."

He sneers at me as he mumbles something under his breath. It takes all my willpower not to burst out laughing, but I enjoy this moment immensely. By the lack of beer breath and it only being a little after five o'clock, there is no way he drank all that beer. He thinks he's clever, but I know he retrieved all those bottles from the recycling bin next to the dumpster.

After Phin throws away the bottles, grumbling the entire time, he grabs the full trash bag and stomps to the front door.

"Wait."

He turns to me with an expression that tells me I have pushed him to his limit.

"There is no way you could have drunk all those beers this afternoon. You didn't, by chance… dig those out of the dumpster, did you?"

His ears turn red as he opens the door. "Pfft. Why would I do a thing like that?"

"You tell me."

Phin marches out of the apartment, and from where I sit, I hear a loud thud of the bag getting tossed into the dumpster. When he comes back inside, he collapses on the couch and lets out a groan. "That backfired."

I snap the recliner shut and stand, placing Dolly on the floor, then wave to his chair. "Your throne awaits. I will be right back."

While I head down the hall, he says, "Take your time."

When I return with my display board, I catch Phin stroking Dolly's chin. I clear my throat, making Phin jump.

Dragging a dining room chair into the living room, I place the display board leaning up against the back of the chair. Opening it, I say, "Since you seem averse to reading the contract, I brought my trusty visual with me."

I open the board filled with all the program's steps on one side and a blank section on the other.

"I read the—"

With my hand, I pop my board, making Phin jump. Phin snaps his mouth shut and swallows hard.

"My program consists of three phases: crate training, socialization, and showcasing. Each step will give you skills to make you the best partner possible."

He scrubs his face with his hands. "I'm a good person. I just haven't found the right person yet."

His soft tone warms my soul, so I purposely smooth my words to keep him on track. "Of course you're a good person, but I want you to be ready when you *do* meet the right person."

Phin takes a deep breath. "Are you in cahoots with my mother? Because that's exactly what she says."

I snort. "No, but many mothers are very appreciative about what I accomplish with their sons."

He rolls his eyes. "Tell me about the first step."

Progress! "Crate training is where you will get comfortable in your own surroundings and make your place homey."

He quirks an eyebrow as Dolly sits at his feet. "Are you talking about throw pillows and candles? Because that's really not my thing. However, if you look under the bathroom counter, I have a few candles left over from women who thought they could tame me." He does a full-body shiver.

"I've noticed. Women don't really care about that stuff, or at least, the right woman won't, especially if it's not natural to you. Speaking of the right woman, tell me about your perfect mate."

He shrugs as he nudges Dolly, trying unsuccessfully to discourage her from lying on his feet. "I like all women. Each one has something to offer, at least for the short term. Some are tall and leggy, a few are voluptuous, most are gorgeous."

I sit on the arm of the couch, mulling over his words. It's apparent he's never had to dig deeper into his feelings. The superficial things have always satisfied him and, in his own words, for the short term. "That's all well and good, but beauty fades."

"That's what Botox is for."

Never mind about progress. He's going to make this as difficult as possible.

"You're willing to fork over four hundred dollars a pop to smooth out some laugh lines? If so, you better be willing to pay for a lot more." I pop him on the leg. "Come on, Phin. Dig deeper, and tell me more than the physical stuff. That's a safe environment. My gut tells me you aren't that shallow."

He chuckles as he scratches the back of his head. "I guess if I put looks aside, I like a woman who is kind."

I write the word "kind" on a strip of paper and thumbtack it to the empty side of my display board. "Go on."

"It's good if she likes some of the same things I do."

I write that down also. "That's good. Similar interests are important. I assume you mean music?"

He nods.

"So she would need to be a fellow musician?"

"Not necessarily but someone who enjoys a good concert—or whose taste doesn't stop at the Jonas Brothers."

I write that down and make a mental note for the hobby session, which might actually combine well with the family meet and greet. He'll love what I have in mind. "Nothing wrong with the Jo Bros, but I get it."

He leans forward, rests his elbows on his knees, and looks off into the distance. "If I'm being honest, I really don't like busybodies. That's a big turnoff."

"No busybodies" gets tacked to my board. "Okay, so no gossipy types. That's good. You're doing great. What about family, religion, politics, stuff like that?"

"Neutral."

This next question will tell me exactly what I'm dealing with, and I hope he can be honest with me. "In the last five years, have you ever had a first date that didn't include sex?"

"Yes. No. I, uh... I don't know."

"Hmmm." I write the word "promiscuous" and tack it to my board.

"When you put it like that..." He lets out a groan. "I like sex. Most men do."

"Completely factual, but love and sex are not usually the same thing, and since a time may come when 'it' doesn't work so well, you better like the person you're with just as much as you like sex."

He glances down at his crotch and back up at me with a pout. "And to think I'm paying for this torture."

"Handsomely, I might add. So, dig deeper. Would it bother you if your partner made more money than you?"

"Nope."

"Makes no money at all?"

"Ha. If she would be happy living in a crappy apartment for the rest of her life, then that's fine with me."

I scribble down my next note and stick it to the board. "Is it important for your family to like your partner?"

"It's just me and Mom, and it would be very important for my mother to like my wife or partner, or whatever, and I guess it's why Mom hasn't met any of my dates in the last few years, at least since I moved out on my own."

My head snaps back as I take in his words. "None?"

"Nope." He pops the *p* in the word.

"One last thing. Tell me about the stash of business cards in the closet."

He blinks a few times. "Did you rifle through my stuff?"

"Not on purpose. I was trying to make room for my stuff. I'm guessing the numbers written on them are from ladies hitting on you. What's with the crumpled ones, and why do you keep them?"

He stiffens, and I can almost see his hackles rising.

"Don't go through my stuff." While I process his defensiveness, he continues. "I'm getting hungry, and I'm tired of being in the hot seat. Want to order a pizza?"

Tonight has been incredibly productive. I've gotten him to open up more than I imagined I would even in the first week, much less the first night, and I certainly don't want to push my luck. Plus, pizza sounds really good right now. The food I ordered can wait until tomorrow.

"Sure. We've covered a lot of ground tonight anyway."

He claps his hands together and jumps out of his chair. "Good. How about a Fantasy pizza from Pizza Perfect?"

Either Phin is a mind reader, or he's done some background checking on me because that is my all-time favorite.

"Order a large. And thank you for being honest with me."

He harrumphs as he stabs at his phone. He may not think so, but this went way better than I imagined it would. And while we wait on the pizza, I slide my phone out of my pocket to make a quick journal entry.

Journal Entry 2

Shocked! He opened up on the first night. I don't know how or why, but I'm thrilled at the breakthrough. I also knew I pushed him to the limit, and it was better to stop with a semi-win than to push his doors closed again. I can easily incorporate his love of music into the family-gathering event. All in all, this session was better than I expected, and I will take any progress from him that I can get.

CHAPTER TEN

Phin

In silence, we chow down on the pizza. The only sound comes from Amelia's dog, who lets out an occasional whimper like she's starving. I pick off a tiny bit of cheese, hoping if Dolly gets something, she will leave us alone.

"I wouldn't do that. She'll be stuck to you like glue if she thinks you hold the keys to the cheese pantry."

"Can't have that, now, can we? Since you had so much fun grilling me, I think turnabout is fair play."

She shakes her head. "That's not how this works."

"Aw, come on. Twenty questions. I'll chop it down to ten."

Her face lights up. "Only because I like this game."

"What made you want to reform men? Don't you think that's a rather unusual profession?"

She stares at the ceiling as she swallows her bite of pizza. I take the opportunity to slip Dolly the dollop of cheese. I wince when Dolly not only bites into the melted goo but takes a hunk of my finger along with it. Dolly licks my hand as if to say thanks and she's sorry for being so eager.

"Well, I just kind of fell into it. What about you? Was your dream job to own a food truck?"

"Hardly. I wanted to be in a rock and roll band, but you know how it is in Nashville. Guitarists are easier to come by than lawyers."

"True. My brother wanted the same but found his niche in the symphony."

Dolly noses me in the shin and lets out a muffled woof.

Amelia narrows her eyes. "Did you...?"

"So, fixing men. Treating them like dogs. What's that all about?"

She snatches the slice of pizza out of my hand and proceeds to bite into it. "I do not treat men like dogs, although some men act worse than canines. I just use similar techniques on men that we use to get dogs ready to be adopted. They really apply."

I scratch my scruffy chin before I snag another slice. "If you had to guess, what dog breed would you think I am? Rottweiler? Powerful and dangerous, or a Labradoodle, goofy and lovable?"

She leans forward and studies my face. Her pale-blue eyes sparkle against her fair skin. I've never been this close to her to fully appreciate the splash of freckles across her nose and cheeks.

"Breed doesn't matter, does it, Dolly?" she asks.

Dolly leans against my leg, and as Amelia mentioned earlier, that critter expects more treats from me.

"But if I had to pick, I guess it would be a poodle."

My slice of pizza slides out of my hand and into my lap. Dolly jumps up on my leg in an attempt to get to the food, but I snatch it up in the nick of time and toss it back on my plate. "I am *not* a poodle. They are all froufrou and high maintenance."

She snickers. "I'm not talking about the miniature version. A standard poodle is very intelligent. They can read their owner's body language, and they love to play. That sounds exactly like you."

Damn, she's good. My brain won't catch up fast enough for me to think of a comeback, so I just point to my hair. "And don't forget this curly mess. Very poodle-ish."

"Trust me, that *is* one of your top ten physical qualities."

My eyebrows raise as her face flames.

"I... uh, thanks? What are the other nine?"

"Not my place to say."

After a long, awkward silence, I clear my throat. "It's getting late. I need to organize my stock for tomorrow's menu."

"Can I help?"

You've helped enough for one day.

"Nope," I blurt as I rise from my chair and collect our paper plates like a good husband. *Gah!* I would have done that even if she weren't here. *I think I would have.* "So, boss lady, did I pass the first step?"

Amelia chuckles as she wipes the table clean of crumbs. "We're just getting started."

"Is it safe to assume we will have more of these deep, thought-provoking conversations in the near future?"

She shrugs as she gathers the pizza box. "I try not to get too deep. Just enough for my clients to get the picture."

"I got the picture, all right. You think I'm a hot mess." I playfully snag the box out of her hand.

She snatches it back. "I never said that."

"You didn't have to." I grab it once more. "I will take this to the dumpster. See? I'm learning already."

She holds up her hands in surrender. "Just don't find any more items there to make a mess of the place."

"Yeah, yeah, yeah."

I walk across the parking lot and toss the box into the metal container, cursing under my breath. I can already feel myself changing, so I need to up my game. *Stat!*

When I return to the apartment, I catch Amelia standing in front of her display board. She posted a large picture of a rough-looking standard poodle that is cut into pieces like a jigsaw puzzle. It looks like something a kindergartner would have drawn.

"Is that me, and did you just happen to have a picture of a poodle lying around?"

She turns and smiles. "Metaphorically speaking, yes. And in my supply cart, I have all sorts of visuals, thanks to my nephew." Amelia touches the image. "Every time you make it through an exercise successfully, I will remove a section of the scruffy pup to reveal a clean, groomed one that has been hiding underneath all along."

She peels off the tail piece to show a manicured one. "You are officially on your way."

"Woof. Don't get any ideas about me being clean-shaven. I like the scruff."

She snickers. "So do I." She slaps a hand over her mouth. "I'll just get this out of the living room, and we can call it a day."

I like seeing her flustered. It's cute. "While you shower, I'll organize the food supplies for tomorrow."

She nods as she drags the display board to her room with me and Dolly right behind her.

I stand in the hallway until she grabs her things for the night and scoots into the bathroom, then I enter her bedroom-slash-food-truck-storage-room. In a hurry, I stuff loaves of bread, buns, an extra jar of pickles, and two massive bags of snack-size chips into a plastic storage bin and arrange them. I move the bin next to my apartment door and give Dolly a warning look. If she gets into my food, she'll never get another piece of cheese from me ever again.

I move as many supplies as I can to the front door because this morning was awkward enough having to step over her while she slept on the air mattress, especially when she rolled over and her bare leg slid out of the covers. I admit I gawked. I can't let that happen again.

Still thinking about her thigh, I make my way to her bedroom and arrange the cold items I will need tomorrow on one easy-to-reach shelf for a quick snatch and run in the morning.

"What's on the menu?"

Her words startle me so much I slam the refrigerator door on my hand. "Oof."

I swing around to find her wearing a pink terry cloth robe that comes to just above her knees, and when she looks down, she jerks the tie closed, but not before I get a peek of her long baggy pink T-shirt with a dog on it—shocker. A rose flush covers her cheeks.

"The usual menu. Mom plans to make some individual chess pies for dessert. Those are always a big hit."

"Save me one?"

"I'll try."

With her eyes trained on the floor, she asks, "Today wasn't so bad, was it?"

I know she wants me to say I learned a lot about myself and that I'll apply the knowledge in the future, but as much as I wanted to resist sharing, the more she prodded, the more truth came out, and that terrified me.

"I guess it could have been worse."

She grins, and if I don't get out of this room, I'm going to embarrass myself.

"Tomorrow will be even more fun."

I let out a chuckle. "We have two very different definitions of fun. Good night, Amelia."

Her name rolls off my tongue too smoothly and easily, like a warm chocolate chip cookie right out of the oven.

"Night."

When I don't make a move to leave her room, she shoos me out. This is going to be harder than I expected. *She's cute and sweet, and...* I don't let myself think anything else. My focus needs to be on winning the bet and nothing more.

I enter the bathroom and do what all men do. I lift the toilet seat, pee without flushing and leave the seat up. That'll show her. And for good measure, I think it's time for a good old-fashioned poker game to really stick in her craw.

While I take the nonperishable items to the food truck, I pull out my phone and call my best friend growing up. Derrick is always game for taking money from willing participants.

"Speak."

"Hey, Derrick. Feel like playing cards tomorrow night?"

"Always. Who will be my next victim?"

"Not sure yet."

"Call Jay. He's such an easy target."

That's not a good idea. He'll see right through my plan to sabotage my bet, so I need to keep him out of it.

"He's too wrapped up in love to hang with us right now. How about you bring your sister?"

Derrick chuckles. "Dude, Layne will rob you blind if given the chance."

"Well, bring her anyway and two of your sloppiest buds. I don't care who. See you at six. I'll order pizza. You bring the cigars and your own beer this time. The last time, you drained my fridge dry."

"Ha. See you then."

I disconnect the phone and almost float back to my apartment. Amelia's going to tsk me about leaving the seat up, but she's going to flip when I bring the boys over for poker, especially after she specifically instructed me against it.

CHAPTER ELEVEN
Amelia

My neck is tighter than a tick from the long day I had. All I want to do is take a nice, long soak in the tub then collapse on my not-so-lovely blow-up mattress. We fostered twenty-four dogs and seventeen cats from one home, and if I had to pick up one more wire crate, I think my arms would have ripped out of my shoulders. My fatigue is a satisfying kind of tired, but after the exhausting, sweaty day I've had, I'm glad to just get back to Phin's apartment to take a hot shower and call it a night.

I pull into Phin's apartment complex, and when I turn into his parking area, all the spaces are filled. I park my car behind Phin's food truck and slog my way to his front door, lugging Dolly inside her carrier. A stereo turned up to the maximum volume rumbles through the parking lot, and I'm glad I have good earbuds so I can drown out the noise while I hit the hay early. Even my mattress on the hard floor will feel amazing tonight. But the closer I get to Phin's apartment, the louder the music is. Oh, no he didn't.

The doorknob vibrates in my hand as I turn it. When I open Phin's door, I'm not sure if the eardrum-bursting stereo or the cigar smoke is worse. Coughing as I enter the apartment, I find Phin with three friends gathered around the kitchen table, playing cards. Phin has a cigar dangling from his mouth as a girl sits so close to him that they could share one chair. He hides his cards close to his chest as he rotates his shoulders away from her.

When he sees me standing there, his eyes grow wide. "Hey!"

Three heads turn to focus on me. The guy with the round face and jet-black hair stuffs his mouth full of chips, crumbs falling onto the floor at his feet.

"Hi." I dare to move a few steps closer to the chaos. Dolly growls from her carrier, and I have to agree. It's definitely a growl-worthy setting.

Phin places his cards facedown on the table and stands as the girl takes the opportunity to raise the corner of one card to sneak a peek at his hand. "You're back early."

I pull out my phone to check the time. "It's almost seven o'clock. Something tells me you assumed I would be gone a little bit longer." I let Dolly loose, and like a bat out of Hades, she scurries into my room.

"Hoped is more like it."

I move toward Phin and step on a chip, turning it into crumbs. "Can I talk to you for a second?"

The side of Phin's mouth turns up. "Sure." He looks at his friends and adds, "Hey, guys, this is Amelia. She's staying with me for a bit."

"Is she your new girlfriend?" the girl asks.

"Nope," Phin and I say at the same time.

The girl grins as her gaze ping-pongs between me and Phin. "I'm Layne, and just to be clear, I'm not his girlfriend either. Never have been, never will be."

"Ouch, but the feeling is mutual," Phin says to her.

"It's a business arrangement," I blurt as my ears radiate heat.

Jet-black-hair dude chuckles and gets a serious stare down by Phin.

With a flat smile, I say to the motley crew, "We'll be right back."

Grabbing Phin by the arm, I drag him through the smoky living room toward the bathroom. I close the door behind us with a click.

He leans against the vanity and grins. "So, how was your day?"

I cross my arms and narrow my eyes at him. "What do you think you're doing?"

"Cards. It's pretty much what I do in my time off. I told you that."

"And I told you that it's not going to happen for a while."

"I don't recall. My bad."

I glance down at the mud-covered floor. "Who did that?"

"That must have been Derrick. He's a landscaper and has a bad habit of tracking in dirt."

"Derrick's the..."

"The tall one."

I poke him in the chest with my finger. "You tell Mr. Green-as-Grass Eyes that he's gross."

"He already knows."

When he takes a step toward the bathroom door to leave, I slide in front of it, blocking his way. Our eyes meet, and we are so close I can feel his breath on my skin. His brow raises as if he's questioning my move. My heart pounds in my ears while I try to find my next words.

To get back into business mode, I throw my shoulders back. "Not yet, mister. We need to go over your contract again. Section three, paragraph four specifically states no fraternizing with 'the boys,' and that out there is a whole bunch of fraternizing. Kennel cough, remember?"

"It's just a simple night with the guys. No harm. And it's what I do." That smug one-shoulder shrug won't get him off the hook.

"Not while you're under contract with me."

"So are you saying you want out of our contract?"

He's not getting out of it so easily. I shake my head and let out a low chuckle. "Oh, I'm not scared off that effortlessly. You have two choices. You either tell the guys—and the girl—good night and clean up that pigsty, or..."

Phin steps closer to me, and his breath tickles on my ear. "Or what, Amelia?"

I jut my chin. "Or plan to lose all your money in the next round of poker."

He guffaws. "Lose to you?"

"Absolutely."

Phin winks. "You're on, sweetheart."

I open the door, and the smoky air accosts me again. "You've been warned."

He has no idea I'm a shark with cards. Phin follows me back into the living room, and I wave to the crew.

"Do you mind if I join your little card game?"

The girl stands, slings an arm around Phin's neck, and whispers in his ear.

He shakes his head. "Stow it, L."

Ugh. He's doing his best to get under my skin and break every rule in the contract all in one night, but he's not going to get rid of me that easily.

"It will be super fun." I hate how flighty my words sound.

Phin claps his hands and clears his throat. "Do any of you have an objection?"

The tall guy with the striking green eyes chuckles as he places his cards facedown on the table. "We would love for Amelia to join us. Right, guys?"

They nod, and the lone girl in the room rolls her eyes.

"Girl, you can have my place," she says. "I've lost enough money tonight anyway. And please, spank them all the way into next week."

"You can count on it."

"Do you even know how to play?" Mr. Green Eyes asks.

"This isn't Go Fish." That came from the other guy, and if he's who left the bathroom like a cesspool, he will pay in spades.

"We play with real money," Phin says.

When I don't answer, the crew quiets down. I snag the cards out of Phin's and the other guys' hands and proceed to shuffle them.

"Hey, that was a good hand."

"Too bad. There's a new sheriff in town." I do a faro shuffle into a cascade, and I hear all the air being sucked out of the room with the gasps.

Under his breath, I hear Phin mumble, "Uh-oh."

Uh-oh is right. *Phin, you have been warned.*

Layne slides onto the kitchen counter and whistles. "This is gonna be fun. My money is on Amelia."

Phin gives her a death stare as he snatches up the cards I dealt him. "Nobody beats me. The odds are always on the house."

I place the remainder of the deck in the middle of the table then arrange my hand. "I live here, too, so..."

I add a wink, making Phin's buddies erupt into laughter. Poor Phin's face is so red I think his head is about to explode.

CHAPTER TWELVE
Phin

Amelia's eyes peek over her hand of cards, and it feels like we are at the shootout at the O.K. Corral. It's eerily quiet in the room as she and I are the last remaining players of this fourth and final round of poker. I thought her perkiness would be a dead giveaway on her hand, but she hasn't given anything away. Not a smirk or an eye twitch or even a raised eyebrow. She's the textbook definition of a poker face.

Derrick enters the room with rubber gloves on his arms up to his elbows. Without taking her eyes off her cards, Amelia asks, "Did you clean up your mess?"

"Yes, ma'am."

"Good. Phin, I believe I called your wager."

"Yes, ma'am, you did. Read 'em and weep." I splay my cards, revealing a beautiful full house. "Sorry, not sorry, darlin'."

Gus rubs his hands together in anticipation while Dolly sits in his lap like they've been buds for years. Layne's eyes twinkle as she stares at me. I don't want to know what she's thinking. Her whispered "You like her" was more than enough.

Amelia's mouth turns down. She sighs then lays out her cards to show a royal flush. All of the oxygen in the room is sucked out by our collective gasps.

She frickin' won the fourth hand. In. A. Row. My blood boils while Amelia looks like a Cheshire cat as she scoops up all our money. Layne cheers her on, and if I didn't know better, I would think they were becoming fast friends. Derrick fumes, and Gus looks a little green around the gills. His wife will never let him come over again.

Amelia belts out the song "Queen of Hearts" by Juice Newton, and it's so off-key that cats in the neighboring county start screeching. Derrick looks like he ran over a skunk while Layne plugs her ears.

Amelia's bellowing echoes throughout the room as she stacks her newly won money in sections based on presidents. "This is fun. One more round?"

"Nooo," Gus says as he stands. "It was nice meeting you. Not really, but you know."

"You too," she says with a bit of sarcasm which nobody else seems to pick up on, which is weird.

Derrick checks his phone. "Yeah, I should go before I owe you my watch."

"Maybe next time?" she asks as she stacks the money in front of her.

He harrumphs.

I show them to the door as Layne chats with Amelia. The guys grumble and stare at their shoes.

"I'll see you guys next week."

Derrick holds his arm out for me to stop talking. "Not a chance. I'm done playing with you. As long as that... that she-devil lives here, I'm staying away." He shakes his head and curses under his breath.

"But..."

I can't get in another word before they stomp out the door and toward their cars.

Layne pats me on the chest and laughs. "You got a live wire with this girlfriend."

"She's not my—"

Layne wags a finger in front of my face. "Whatever, dude. Nice meeting you, Amelia."

"You too. Lunch soon?"

"You got it."

What just happened?

I close the door with a loud click and lean against it, waiting for Amelia to stop her counting. When she looks up, she asks, "What?"

Sneering, I say, "You know what. Are you Doyle Brunson's grand-daughter or something?"

"Ha. No. I just have ruthless siblings."

"I believe you."

She picks up her massive wad of cash and stares at the stack for a moment while she nibbles on her bottom lip. After a deep breath, she rushes toward me and shoves the bills into my hands then says, "Give this back to your friends. I don't want the money. I mean, I *do* need—I mean, want—it, but I can't keep it. I just wanted to teach *you* a lesson."

"Oh yeah? And what is that?"

"That this lifestyle isn't going to do you any favors for finding your soulmate."

"I like my friends and my... lifestyle."

Amelia stands toe to toe with me, and I get a whiff of peach lotion.

"Your commitment to the contract—"

Grumbling, I say, "I know. Fine."

"And you let them go without cleaning up the place."

"Derrick cleaned up the bathroom, but I'll straighten the rest an-other day."

She shakes her head. "We will clean together. I think I made your friends mad, so the least I can do is help clean up and get the smoky smell out of here." She gags. "How do you manage it? It's gross."

The last thing I want to do is agree with her, because she irritates the heck out of me. She was supposed to get all huffy and leave and take her crazy dog and stupid contract with her. But instead, she won all our money and made friends with Layne, all with a smile on her face.

Amelia cranks up the tunes on her phone, and when "Stairway to Heaven" begins, I ask her, "What album featured this song?"

She scrunches her nose as she thinks. "*Led Zeppelin III*?"

I punch my fist with elation that I've beaten the trivia queen. "Nope, it's *IV*."

She groans as she crosses her arms over her chest with a huff. "Are you sure? Because they were produced only a year apart."

"While I'm impressed you knew the release dates, I'm still stoked I got you at your own game, especially after that major loss with cards."

"Pfft. This time."

As the two of us straighten up the living room, I replay the look on Gus's face when he lost his last dollar.

"What's so funny?"

I shrug. "Just thinking of Gus and what kind of hot water he's probably in right now."

"He only lost about thirty dollars, so I can't imagine he's in too much trouble." She stuffs the trash can full of pizza boxes and dumps the ashtray. "Yuck. Do you make this kind of mess when you go to their houses?"

"They always come here."

Amelia rolls her eyes while she puts the cards back into the holder. "Well, duh. They don't want to mess up their own homes. Do you blame them?"

"I never thought of it that way. I figured I was doing them a favor. Gus has a baby at home. Can't very well be loud and smoke cigars around that."

"What about Derrick?" She wipes the table clean and returns the chip containers to the cupboard. "I didn't get the impression he was married."

My eyebrows raise. "Oh. If you are interested in him, I can set you up."

She holds her hands out in front of her. "Nope. Not my type. I was actually thinking he might be a good candidate for whenever I'm done with you, that is, *if* I'm ever done with you."

I pause, wondering what she means by "if" she's done with me. It doesn't look like I'm going to get rid of her anytime soon, so I might as well play along and act as if I'm on board with her silly procedures. Anything to win that guitar.

"I'll be ready to meet my future forever mate before you know it."

"I don't know," she singsongs. "If tonight is any indication, we have a lot to work on."

Clutching my chest, I fake like her words hurt. "Harsh, Lia."

She freezes, and her big brown eyes grow even bigger. Blinking a few times, she whispers, "What did you just call me?"

"Uh... I think it was Lia. I'm sorry if that was inappropriate or too casual."

She stares down at her shoes and shakes her head. "It's okay. It just... nothing." She shakes her head again. "Never mind. You may call me whatever you want."

If some dude gave her a cute pet name then stomped all over her heart, I feel like seeking him out and punching him in the nose. Yes, she's obnoxious with her dog references and her perpetual chipper attitude, but all of it is starting to grow on me. And if it hurts her, I will never use that nickname again.

I step closer to her and take the trash bag from her hands. She crosses her arms over her chest as her gaze ping-pongs around the room.

"Amelia, I won't call you that again if it makes you sad."

Our eyes meet, and her expression is full of hope and wonder. "Really?" She bites her lip. "That's very sweet."

The way she stares up at me makes me want to take a step toward her and see what those lips feel like on mine. Out of the corner of my eye, I see my guitar collection and am reminded of the bet with Jay. If I cross the line with Amelia, I'll lose.

Clearing my throat and my fuzzy brain, I motion toward the front door. "Let's take the trash out and call it a day. I'm pooped... and broke."

She hip bumps me as we walk down the sidewalk toward the apartment dumpster. I carry the bag while she holds the carton of beer bottles for the recycling bin.

"I won't take your money if you admit one thing."

"And what is that?"

"That even something as mundane as cleaning the apartment is much more pleasant with someone by your side."

"Maybe."

"See, that wasn't so hard to admit, was it?"

As if in slow motion, her foot catches on the uneven sidewalk, sending the beer bottles to the pavement with a crash and her right on top of them. She lands with a thud, but not before her hand slides across one of the jagged pieces of glass.

She gasps then lets out a string of made-up curse words. "Flibbit, fork it, fudge-a-mania."

I help her to her feet and notice the trail of blood running down her arm. This is not good.

CHAPTER THIRTEEN
Amelia

Phin drags me into his apartment and leads me toward the sink. He turns on the faucet and shoves my hand under the water. I suck in a breath as pain sears through my finger while blood drips into the sink. He wraps a paper towel around my finger, and blood soaks through immediately.

"This isn't good. Hold your finger high, and keep pressure on it. I'll get the first aid kit."

He runs out of the kitchen, and I hear the water in the bathroom turn on. Then, I hear a few cabinet doors slamming before his footsteps race back into the kitchen.

"Sorry. I needed to wash the dumpster grime off my hands. Let me see what you've done."

My hand shakes as he guides me to the kitchen table. He scoots a chair next to mine, and I feel his breath on me while he pulls out the supplies from his first aid kit.

When he removes the blood-soaked napkin, his eyes flick toward mine. "Amelia, I think you're going to need stitches."

My lunch threatens to make a repeat appearance. "I'll be fine."

I stand quickly, and the ground tilts. Right before I hit the floor, Phin scoops me up and plants me on the couch. He puts two pillows under my feet and grabs a towel out of the kitchen. Dolly must think it's snuggle time, because she jumps onto my stomach and circles to get comfortable.

Phin picks her up and plunks her on the floor. "Not now, critter."

She scurries off toward my bedroom.

While he wraps my hand with the towel, he shakes his head. "It's pretty deep. I'll drive you."

"You don't have to do that. I'll call an Uber."

He snorts as he stands. Phin scoops up his keys and helps me to a stand. "I may not be good husband material, but I am a good person. I refuse to let you take yourself. My mother would kick my butt if I did that. ER or urgent care? It's your call."

"Whichever is prepared to perform a hand transplant."

He slides a hand down my face. "I'm not a doctor, but I'm pretty sure you won't need that today."

I hold on to his waist with my good hand like my life depends on it as we make our way to the door. "What about my dog?"

He pauses as if he doesn't know how to answer. "If she poops in the house, I'll clean it up. Or do you want me to crate her?"

"She's probably hiding under the bed right now. I think she'll be fine. In hindsight, maybe we should have just left the place a mess so we wouldn't have to worry about a doggy accident."

Phin chuckles. "See? I was forward-thinking."

"Don't make me laugh." I suck in a breath at the pain.

While he walks me outside, I sneak a peek at the towel around my hand. Bad idea. A bit of blood starts to seep through, making my stomach turn. Thank goodness he doesn't take me to his food truck, because if I had to smell grease right now, I would throw up. Instead, he opens the door to a clunker of a truck that has seen better days, and I think I might be better off, and safer, if I walk to get my finger tended to.

As I settle into the passenger seat, he leans over to latch my seat belt, and when our eyes meet, he smiles.

"Is this part of phase one?"

I rest my head on the headrest as a tear trickles down my cheek, but laughter bubbles out of my throat. "Definitely not. I would never cause myself pain. I can't say the same for you, though."

"Ha. Not surprised." He brushes the tear away with his thumb then jerks his hand away as if my skin stung him. He swallows. "Let's get you taken care of."

My lunch starts to make its way up my throat, so I roll my window down. The cool breeze helps decrease my nausea.

"You okay over there?"

I do a thumbs-up then turn my thumb down. Between shallow breaths, I eke out, "Talk to me. Otherwise, I may puke."

"Hey, eyes on me." He snaps his fingers under my nose to get my attention.

I do as he instructs and notice the concern etched across his face.

He clears his throat. "Who was the first woman inducted into the Rock and Roll Hall of Fame?"

I rack my brain, but the pain in my hand keeps me from focusing. "I don't know."

"Sure, you do. Think." When I don't reply, he sings in a falsetto voice the lyrics to "A Natural Woman."

"Please, don't do that. You sound worse than me, and we both know that's pretty bad."

He sucks in a breath between his teeth. "I can honestly say I have never heard a voice like that before."

"Not funny."

At the stoplight, he inspects my hand. He grimaces when he sees the towel getting redder. "Looks good."

"You're a terrible liar."

When the traffic light turns green, he replies, "I'll take that as a compliment."

He yammers on and on about music the entire trip to the hospital, anything to keep my mind occupied. At every light, he reinspects my hand and nods, like he's trying to convince himself it's not too bad. Phin is more complex than he wants to let on. He's definitely not as one-dimensional as he wants to portray. The way his jaw clenches as he maintains a death grip on the steering wheel makes me think he doesn't like people seeing the softer side of Phin.

"Thanks for driving me. That is very sweet of you."

"I can't have you bleeding all over my apartment, right?"

"I guess not."

"I'm sorry."

"No need. These things happen."

He brushes hair out of my eyes, and that one simple act sets every one of my nerve endings on fire. No one's touch has done that to me in a very long while, and now is not the time. I have a job to do. My stupid girlish hormones need to calm it down. He would do this for anyone. He's my client, and I should appreciate the fact that he hasn't used this incident to back out of the contract, at least for now. But I need this client way more than he needs me.

CHAPTER FOURTEEN
Phin

"You doing all right over there?" I ask as I switch lanes.

She breathes in and out like she's doing some kind of yoga exercise then closes her eyes. "Not really. I don't do well with blood. And there was so much. All over the..." Her eyes widen, and her cheeks puff like she's got a mouthful of something.

"Do I need to pull over?"

She nods, and I turn on a dime, cutting off a truck in the right lane before I come to a screeching halt in a strip mall parking lot. Amelia flings open the door, and before I can jump out and run around to help her, she springboards onto the grassy area, spewing everything she had to eat.

While she retches a few more times, I rummage through my truck in search of paper towels. Doing my best not to focus on the puke on the ground, I shove some napkins under her nose.

"Thanks." She wipes her face and holds up her hand with the blood-soaked bandage. "Oh, no. More—"

"I've got this." I lead her back to the truck and strap her in. "I doubt you'll yak anymore, so that's good."

She chuckles. "Stop doing that."

"Put pressure on your hand and hold it high. We'll be at the urgent care in a few minutes if I don't hit every red light."

"Not soon enough."

"Not to downplay your condition, but I don't think it's very deep. I think it's cut at an angle, making it hard to stop the bleeding." I remember when I first decided to go into the food industry. "You see this?" I shove my left hand in her face. "First casualty of my food truck career. I got that scar from cutting carrots." I push up my sleeve to show her my arm. "That scar is from leaning against a hot stove. And this..." I pull down the neck of my T-shirt. "Never work around hot grease without a shirt."

Amelia snorts, and for some reason, it makes me grin that I could distract her.

She places her feet on the dashboard and stares out the window. "I'm really sorry."

As I turn into the urgent care center, I glance at her. "Look at it this way. If you ever want to go into the food truck business, you have your inaugural battle scar already out of the way, even if it was broken glass. I won't tell anyone."

"I'll stick to working with dogs."

I quirk an eyebrow. "Did you just call me a dog?"

"Truth hurts."

"Ouch."

After helping her to the door and getting her settled into a chair, I go in search of water for her. Walking down the hallway, looking for a vending machine, I pass two extremely beautiful nurses in those cute form-fitting scrubs. They smile at me, and if I weren't on a mission to get Amelia something to drink, I would have started a conversation with them and gotten at least one phone number out of the convo.

I purchase the water and head back to the waiting area just as Amelia is called back to a room. I hold the bottle out to her. "I'll be out here waiting for you. Don't puke anywhere."

She takes the bottle from me, her hand brushing against mine. "Thanks, but... I don't want to be alone."

"Okay." I follow her, and she pulls out her cell phone, using her un-injured hand. "Would you call one of my sisters or my brother for me?"

"Sure. Why not your parents?"

"I don't want to worry them, but just in case I need a pint of blood, I want someone related to me on standby."

I throw my head back and laugh then scroll through her unlocked phone for numbers. "You haven't lost that much blood."

"You never know."

My eyebrows scrunch as I review names in her contact list. "Axel is your brother, right?"

"Yes. Call him. He's the least dramatic of the crew."

While the nurse assesses Amelia's cut, I dial the number.

"Speak."

"Uh... is this Axel?"

"Yup," comes the gruff reply.

"I am a... I'm at the Bellevue Medical Center on Broad Street with your sister, Amelia."

"Is she okay?"

"She's fine, she just cut her finger pretty badly, so she wanted me to call you."

"Who are you?"

"I'm Phin. I'm her..."

"Oh, her client. Wait a sec. What did you do to her?"

"Nothing. She cut her hand on a broken bottle."

"Hmm. Something tells me you haven't been housebroken yet."

"Your sister is strange."

"You're telling me," he replies.

Amelia perks up. "Hey, I heard that."

"Tell her I'm just leaving the performance hall."

"Okay."

I disconnect, and I'm left staring at Amelia's phone. I hand it back to her. "Your brother is on the way. What else can I do?"

Amelia takes deep breaths, and I hope she's not going to yak again.

"Nothing, thank you. I usually limit how many times a client meets my family, but this was unexpected. On the plus side, I got to see how you handle a crisis, even though this was obviously not part of the plan."

"How'd I do?"

"Looks like you get to remove another piece of that scruffy poodle."

No matter the situation, she's constantly thinking about the contract. I stare at her for the longest time until she offers the cutest bashful smile. I bust out a laugh at how ridiculous that sounds.

She rolls her eyes. "Everything should be fine as long as Axel doesn't call one of my sisters. Things could get pretty out of control if they all get involved. My family can be... over the top."

I probably don't want to know what that means.

Amelia and I wait in a corner of the lobby while the hospital staff completes her paperwork. This takes longer than the entire procedure to clean and close up the wound. Luckily, though her injury was deep, it didn't hit any nerves or tendons, and she should heal quickly. The doctor used some sort of superglue on her hand, so she should be as good as new in a few days and probably won't even have a scar.

Multiple voices from down the hallway get louder, and I hear a ruckus.

Amelia's jaw drops. "Oh no."

Lots of people jabber all at one time.

"Where is she? I need to see her chart."

"Is she dead yet? Mom is going to be so upset."

"I'm her power of attorney. I demand to know what's going on."

Amelia groans and leans over the arm of her seat to see where the noise is coming from. "Guys, stop your yapping."

I stand, but before I can get one step closer to the door, a mob of people shoving their way toward Amelia push me back. Three women who resemble Amelia and one shaggy-headed beatnik of a dude take over the space. I do my best to blend into the wall.

The tallest blonde examines Amelia's hand. "Sis, I think you'll live this time."

The smallest blonde plops into the chair next to Amelia and puts an arm around Amelia's shoulders. "They didn't overdo it just to charge you more, did they?"

"I don't know. And what are you all doing here?" She stares at the guy. "Could you not come alone?"

He saunters over to her and cocks his head to the side as he checks her hand. "And miss out on the fun as these three mother hens interrogate your new client-slash-boyfriend?"

Five sets of eyes laser in on me, and I wish I could teleport myself out of the room.

I'm kicking my butt for sticking around. I hold up my hands like I'm under arrest. "That is not what's going on here."

Amelia stands when her name is called to complete her paperwork. "He is *not* my boyfriend. He's my next client."

Now three sets of eyes pin the beatnik dude in place, and the smallest woman pokes his chest. "You said he was her boyfriend."

"Potato, puh-tah-to."

I hold out my hand to shake his. "Sorry for the confusion. But for clarification, I'm not her boyfriend. I'm her client."

The girl sitting next to Amelia does a full-body scan and grins. "We can fix that."

Clumsily, Amelia hands the clerk her credit card. The clerk stares at it for a moment before she slides it into the machine to pay.

"He's my foster husband. You know the drill. Phin, these are my over-the-top, meddling siblings. Ramona, Laura, Dorothy, and Axel. Guys, this is Phin. Sorry. You weren't supposed to meet them for another couple of days, but here we are."

I wave, and for the first time, I can't form words.

One of her sisters says, "Dang, sis. How do you find the hottest clients?"

Amelia focuses on holding her injured hand up while trying to sign the receipt with her other. My ears burn, and if I didn't want that guitar so bad, I would back out of the contract right now. When I agreed to have a woman share my space, I didn't expect it to include her entire inquisitive family too. If I spend any more time with them, I can probably expect to be hooked up to a lie detector machine and interrogated. No wonder Amelia is still single.

CHAPTER FIFTEEN
Amelia

My head spins from all the chatter in the waiting area as I try to figure out how I'm going to pay for this visit. I'll now have a medical bill collector hounding me at every turn. Thank goodness the billing person agreed to let me pay for the office visit now and bill me for the rest. Ramona, my sweet nurse sister, inspects my wound, making Laura dry heave. Dorothy rattles on and on to my mother over the phone about my situation and that I won't die this time. Axel and Phin jabber about something musical, and I'm at least relieved that they have some camaraderie in such an estrogen-filled space.

Not being able to take any more, I yell, "Guys!"

Everyone stops chattering to stare at me, even the ten other families scattered throughout the waiting area.

"I appreciate all your support and concern, but it's obvious I am not going to cash in my chips today. We can all go home now."

One by one, my sisters file toward the exit.

Axel pops Phin on the back before leaving. "See you at the concert."

I wish he hadn't said that.

"Come again?" Phin asks, scrunching his brow.

I shoo Axel out of the room and say to Phin, "I'll explain later."

We stare at each other. The only sound is the buzz of the fluorescent bulbs.

To break the silence, I say, "Welcome to a day in the life of the Day family."

He chuckles as he helps me from the waiting area and out to his truck. All the while, he has my purse slung over his shoulder. He leaves so much unsaid in that sexy rumble from his throat, but I'm terrified to ask. I give him two extra points for being secure enough in his masculinity to carry my purse in public.

"I may need the poker winnings after all, to pay for this little outing."

"Ah, insurance will cover most of it, right?"

I shrug because I lost my health insurance with my last job. My volunteer gig doesn't offer it, and thinking of how much this injury is going to cost me makes me bite my lip to keep from crying.

We ride back to Phin's apartment, and my hand is already starting to throb. I refused narcotics because I didn't want a repeat performance of upchucking all over myself. I only hope Phin has some OTC meds I can take. All I have is Dolly's heartworm prevention pills, and I seriously doubt I should take anything prescribed for a canine unless I need deworming.

Unable to take the silence anymore, I blurt out my apology. "I'm sorry about cutting my hand and... my siblings."

He shrugs. "Can't pick your family."

"I mean, you weren't supposed to meet them like this."

Phin gulps, his Adam's apple bobbing. "They're a lot to handle, that's for sure, but I don't believe you would do any of this on purpose."

"Of course I wouldn't do that. Even *you* aren't worth that kind of pain." I give him a cheesy grin.

He scrubs his face as he turns a corner. "I think I should get two sections of the poodle removed."

I roll my eyes. "You didn't have to come to begin with, so you will get one extra. That is all." I stare out the window, my head throbbing more than my hand. "I think I need to let you out of your contract. This is not going to work."

He snaps his head around so fast he swerves on the road. "What? No."

There he goes again, flip-flopping between acting like he wants out and practically begging to stay in. With a grumpy snarl, he snaps his head back to the road.

"Oh, so you want to continue now? That's a change of heart."

Phin mumbles something then lets out a breath. "I'm sorry I've made things difficult for you from the get-go. The mess I made intentionally, the poker game, which you came out of smelling like a rose... all of it. I will try to do better."

"Thank you. But even if you just met most of my family, you will still have the planned event later to meet the 'rents too."

He gives me an adorable smile that I'm sure makes all the girls swoon, and I have to admit, it's very effective. "I was hoping we could check that one off the list."

I bite my lip as I shake my head. "Sorry, dude. They were in panic mode today. I want you to see them in their normal state."

He snorts. "Somehow, I feel like nothing about you or your family is normal."

If it weren't true, I would be insulted. I roll my eyes. "Normal is highly overrated in my opinion."

"Yeah. Normal is boring, and you..." He pinches me on the cheek. "You are far from boring."

I stare out the window in hopes he doesn't see the cherry-red flush across my face.

After a beat of silence, he says, "Hold on a sec. Your brother said something about a concert."

Examining my bandage, I say, "That's part of the hobby phase. While you technically will meet the family there, the main purpose is to observe you doing one of your favorite things."

His eyebrows waggle. "Do I get to pick the concert?"

"No."

"Buzzkill."

When we arrive back at his apartment, he unlocks the door, and Dolly does her gotta-pee dance around my legs.

"Okay, girl. I know."

It takes Dolly about a nanosecond to do her business on the lawn, and her tail wags like crazy in appreciation. When I return to Phin's apartment, he's placing a sheet over the couch and fluffing a pillow.

He sees me and freezes. "What? I didn't think you would be comfortable sleeping on the air mattress with your injury, so you can take my bed, and I'll sleep on the couch." He blushes as he flops out a blanket.

Phin blushes! How cute.

I gulp at the kind gesture. "That's very sweet of you, but I will not be sleeping in your bed, with or without you. It clearly states in the contract, no sex... or sleeping... besides, your bed probably smells like you. I think I'm going to stop talking now." *Open mouth, insert foot.*

Phin's jaw drops, and he lets out a deep, husky chuckle then shakes his head as if he's trying to remove his thoughts. "Okay." He motions to the couch. "Your bed awaits, my lady."

I plop down on the couch and bounce, making Dolly jump up in my lap. "Not bad."

He retrieves two water bottles from the kitchen and hands me one then sits in his recliner and takes a sip from his bottle. "It's obvious I did not read the contract, so give me the movie-trailer version of housetraining. That sounds very demeaning."

I clear my throat as I prop my injured hand on a pillow. "It certainly isn't meant to be disrespectful at all. My program includes four very important categories. Health and wellness, behavior, showcasing, and finally, HEA."

"HEA?"

"Yeah. Happily ever after. Finding your forever home."

He scratches the back of his head. "Yeah, I don't think I'm wired like that."

"Everyone is, but first, we must tackle the basic house-training items. You have to be comfortable being alone in your own space. You have to learn how to stay away from fleas and parasites."

Phin's eyebrows raise. "I do *not* have fleas."

I giggle. "Of course not. Fleas are girls who are always hanging around. Parasites are women who are trying to hook you for the wrong reasons."

He spews water from his mouth. Coughing to extract it from his lungs, he leans over to fist-bump me. "That is spot-on."

Pride swells inside me from his acknowledgment of my analogy. "Then, there's kennel cough, which for a human, is other dudes trying to keep you a bachelor. You know, the guys who you routinely either go to sports bars with or play poker. You have to avoid them until you are immune. Hint, hint. Mr. Green Eyes."

"I like my friends. I'm not sure I want to give up my so-called kennel cough."

I get this pushback every time, so I'm prepared with a canned response. "Until you see what it's like to be free of the *cough*, you won't know how bad you feel right now."

He harrumphs, downs the last of his water, then without another word, he enters the bathroom. The door closes with a click, and the shower rumbles on. Dolly curls up behind the crook of my knee and lets out a breath indicating she is settled in for the night. I scratch her head as I drift off to sleep.

Phin is going to be one of the hardest clients I've worked with. He acts all tough, but then his softer side kicks in on autopilot before he can stop himself. It's like the real Phin is a good guy and would make someone a great husband, but something is holding him back. I would hate for him to miss out on all the joys of a committed relationship. I know I can assist him to be comfortable with who he really is. It may take a lot of work and a ton of patience, but I'm up for the challenge.

Journal Entry 3

Phin Baxtor is a complex client who, on the surface, appears to be very satisfied with his bachelorhood. He enjoys flirting with every female, expresses that he likes being single, and verbally resists the contract. However, almost like a switch, he changes over to a caring person very capable of being an ideal husband. One would think it's an act, but which part? The flirty party boy or the thoughtful putting-others-first guy?

If he hadn't been a referral, I would not have taken on this client. After one day, I already know he's going to bend every rule and make each step more difficult than it has to be. It's as if he is trying to sabotage the entire plan, even though he agreed to and paid for the service.

My accident and the subsequent meeting of my family was not intentional, but they turned out to be beneficial. He stepped up to the plate to help me and even didn't make me sleep on the blow-up mattress with an injury. And he got a glimpse into what an intruding family is like. I intend to move forward with the hobby event and will insert the standard meet-the-family step during stage two. By that time, I should have figured out his intentions.

Phin Baxtor will be husband material by the time I am finished with him.

CHAPTER SIXTEEN
Phin

It had been hard enough knowing Amelia was sleeping right across the hall from me, but at least an extra door had been between us. Tonight, she's on the couch, sacked out with her hand resting on a pillow. I wouldn't know the part about the pillow or that she sleeps with her mouth open if I hadn't found every excuse in the book to check on her. This time, it's to make sure the air conditioner isn't blowing right on her.

Lame.

And that mangy mutt keeps eyeing me as if to warn me off from coming any closer. I hold up my hands in surrender as if Dolly knows what that means. When I take a step away, she settles back in behind Amelia's knee.

I guzzle water and tiptoe back through the living room, when my foot catches on her purse, the same one that I carried a few hours earlier, and I am sent sailing across the room, crashing into the wall.

Amelia pops her head up and looks at me. "You okay?"

As I crawl to a standing position, hoping all my digits are intact, I say, "Mm-hm. Little toe."

With a groan, she sits up and catches me hopping around. "Ouch."

"God, that hurts." I collapse into a chair and count to ten.

She yawns. "My father says the only purpose for the little toe is to find things in the dark."

I belt out a laugh. "Truer words were never spoken. I didn't mean to wake you. I just went to get a glass of water and didn't want to turn on the light."

"You must be one thirsty dude because that is at least the fourth time you've come in here."

Busted. I focus on my toe, even though it barely hurts anymore. "I, uh... just didn't want you to be uncomfortable out here."

She snorts as she adjusts herself on the couch. "And was that your thought process when you set me up on the air mattress?"

Busted again. Scratching the back of my head, I try to come up with a logical reply, but I am at a loss. "Of course."

Amelia pets Dolly on the head and lies back down with a large yawn. "I'm sorry to tell you this, but the blow-up mattress is not that bad. I might get one after our contract is up."

"If you like that one so much, I'll gift it to you."

She clutches her chest. "Aww, so sweet."

"How is your hand?"

"In pain but not terrible if I don't roll over on it."

"That's good. I'm glad you're okay."

"Me too." She lets out another yawn and rolls over. "Good night, Phin."

Watching her snuggle into her pillow does something to me that I don't think I like. Maybe it's because I've never had a woman sleep over the entire night. I'm the one who usually does the walk of shame, and I like it that way. Watching Amelia let out a sleepy sigh is exactly why I do what I do. I'm a huge sucker for the simple things, but as long as I keep those away and focus on flashy, superficial women instead, I'm not tempted to dig deeper into a relationship.

"Why are you still here?"

Her words snap me out of the psychoanalysis of my love life. "Yeah, heading out right now."

I purposefully stare at the ceiling until I'm down the hallway and safely inside my bedroom. I snatch my phone off my nightstand and plop down on the bed to scroll through my social media feed that, luckily, I have only used to promote the business. Even so, tons of ego-boosting comments from gorgeous women in town for bachelorette parties say they want that "hottie in a food truck" to hang out with them. *Blech.* Even though I enjoy them when they show up at the truck, what I love is that they spend money that goes into my pocket, not the reverse. I love women, but ruining a bride-to-be's reputation, which is what a lot of the partygoers are hoping to do, is not my thing.

I see that Layne is online, so I message her.

Me: *Sorry Amelia ruined the fun.*

Layne: *Are you kidding? She is awesome.*

Me: *Annoying is more like it.*

Layne: *Aww… someone's gotta crush.*

Heat works up my neck, and I think my ears are on fire. That is not what is going on here. At. All.

Me: *I don't do crushes. You know that. How long have we known each other?*

Layne: *Diapers? Mud pies? Hard to remember. Just be honest about one thing.*

I groan as I contemplate just turning off my phone and forgetting I started this stupid conversation.

Layne: *Hello???*

Me: *What?*

Layne: *You think she's cute.*

It's better to own it and make light of it so she'll leave me alone. If I deny it, she'll never stop.

Me: *Of course I think she's cute. Who wouldn't?*

Bad idea. I know better than to add a question. That will only continue this conversation, and it won't end well.

Layne: *Typically, you think a girl is gorgeous, beautiful, and most of the time, you use the description "hot" but never cute. You like this girl, and you don't want to admit it.*

Sometimes, having long-term friends really sucks. Layne reads me like a book, and it's terrifying how well she can get into my brain with one simple choice of words.

Me: *Nope.*

Layne: *Liar. Cute is endearing.*

Me: *Cute is cute. Teddy bears are cute.*

Layne: *Do you think I'm cute?*

I belt out a laugh and hope I didn't wake up Amelia.

Me: *Not at all. I think you are annoying.*

Layne: *I'll take that as a compliment. Don't be afraid of something deeper than a one and done.*

I cringe at her choice of words.

Me: *You suck.*

Layne: *And that is why I am the unofficial sister you never had. Night.*

Me: *Later.*

I turn off the phone and rest my arm under my head while I stare at the ceiling. A small possibility exists that I think Amelia is cute, and maybe even more than that, and it scares the crap out of me.

CHAPTER SEVENTEEN
Amelia

Every time I turn over on the couch, a pain shoots through my hand. Thoughts of the previous day run through my mind, and even though things didn't go exactly as planned—the poker game, the injury, the family meeting Phin too early—it wasn't a complete disaster.

I reread my text messages from last night. The subtle shift in my reclining position causes Dolly to stand and shake.

Layne: *Nice to meet you. You kicked their butts. Way 2 go!*

Me: *It was fun.*

Layne: *So, you're really going to attempt a Phin transformation?*

Me: *Yep. That's what I do.*

Layne: *Good luck. No woman has ever been able to pin him down for more than a week. Not that I've ever tried, because...*

Me: *I am good at what I do.*

My phone pings again, and I have to blink a few times when I see Axel's name pop up as the caller. He's never called me before ten o'clock. Ever.

"Hey, why are you up so early? I thought musicians slept until noon every day."

"Ha ha. I wanted to make sure you're okay."

"I'm better." I hold my hand out in front of me and examine the bandaging. "I won't be playing the piano anytime soon, but I'll live."

"As if you could play the keys to begin with."

"Ha. You're so funny." My sarcasm drips from my words. "Shouldn't you be resting up for your concert?"

"After a quick rehearsal, I'm going to take a nice, long nap. Speaking of the concert, are we still on for tonight? Phin acted clueless."

"That's because he didn't know. I only make my clients aware of what's next in the steps, or they get overwhelmed. So if you set me back, I will never let you live it down."

"I know. I'm the worst, but I didn't know and don't care about the way your mind works. That is one scary place."

I rise and head to the front door to let Dolly do her business. "Not cool, bro."

"I know your new BFF will like it. I'm emailing you the tickets. Bye."

Before I can protest, he disconnects the call. Dolly stares at me like she's waiting for me to read my email, so I sit on the curb while she enjoys a moment in the morning sun.

"Come on, girl. Let's catch Phin before he leaves," I say, heading inside. With my head down, reading more about the concert, I run into a wall of muscles.

"Consider me caught."

"Hey." My voice is all breathy and annoying.

"Good morning." His voice is nice and gravelly and way too sexy.

As usual, his curly hair flips over the edge of his ball cap as he slogs past me and into the kitchen. He starts a pot of coffee, and while the delicious dark liquid drips into the carafe, he leans against the counter and closes his eyes. When it's done brewing, he lets out a deep purr while he fills two cups and hands one to me.

As I snatch the cup from him, I drop my phone. "Oops."

He picks it up and cocks his head when he reads the sender of the last text message. "You're chatting with Layne?"

"She seems like a fun person to hang with."

He grumbles as he sips his coffee. "Fun like a hangover. But she's my oldest friend, so I can't just ditch her now."

"As if you would."

Phin mulls over my words. "So, what have you got planned to torture me with today?"

"Well, actually..."

"Does this have anything to do with what your brother said last night?"

"My brother is playing in the symphony tonight. I've got tickets. Since you're a musician, I thought it would fit into the hobby piece of the plan."

He cringes. "Classical? That's not actually my style of music."

"I knew you would say that, but this is a very unusual concert. It's all Beatles music."

He quirks an eyebrow. "Seriously?"

"Yep, and it's way cool. Last year, they did *Star Wars*, and it was amazing."

Phin chews his lip, and I sense that he's trying to find a way to say no, but it's the Beatles, and I know how much every musician loves everything about the Fab Four.

"Do I have to wear a tux?"

Thoughts of him dressed in a fancy black suit pop into my mind, his curly hair touching the collar of his crisp white dress shirt. I sigh and let my mind wander to where the top button is undone, exposing a trickle of chest hair. *Oh God...*

"Amelia? You still here?"

I jump and wonder how long I was daydreaming. *Amelia, pull yourself together. It's part of the program, not a date, remember?* "Oh. You can wear a tux if you want, but it's not required. Most people dress nice, but for these kinds of concerts, people wear anything from formal to almost hobo-ish."

"What are you going to wear?"

I shrug. "Probably a sundress."

He turns to me, his eyes sparkling, then his mouth twitches up into a smile. "Okay, Miss Day. It's a date." He takes a step backward and bumps into the wall. "Not a date-date, but a... you know."

"I know, silly." Heat radiates up my neck, and I'm sure it's all splotchy. The idea of going on a date with him makes my stomach feel all gushy. I clear my throat.

Phin tweaks my nose. "It's a nondate. See you this afternoon."

I watch him swagger to his food truck, and I'm already worried about how this is going to play out. Usually, the hobby segment doesn't include my family, and the family meet and greet is something more casual. Still, my brother's concert is a good way to see how he reacts out of his comfort zone but with a slice of something he likes. Phin will do fine. I'm not so sure about myself. This is going to be a very long day and an even longer evening.

CHAPTER EIGHTEEN

Phin

Jay's entire body trembles with laughter, and I pop him in the stomach, making him let out an oof. "She asked you out on a date?"

I keep my head buried so he can't see my flushed face. "It's not a date. It's part of the program. A musical function, and you know as well as I do that if you were in my shoes, you would want to go too. It's a tribute to the Beatles. How bad could it be?"

"Hazel says Amelia's brother is an amazing cellist. Pretty much a musical prodigy, lucky jerk."

Suddenly, the most brilliant idea pops into my mind. I do a mental kick to my butt for not thinking of this earlier. If I have to endure Amelia's program, I might as well get something out of it. "He should join our band."

Jay guffaws. "Dude, he's musically at a totally different level than we are. He's a professional. We're still at the high school garage band stage. In fact, I wouldn't consider us a band. We're just two guys who get together to jam occasionally." He pops me on the back.

I point a spatula at him while I make a BLT sandwich. "Hey, you never know until you ask, and one of us has a really cool vintage guitar. Just saying."

Jay chuckles. "Yes, I do, and it will continue to be mine for a very long time."

"Don't count on it. Amelia thinks I'm doing great."

He stares a hole through me. "She said that?"

I bury my head while I work on the next order. "Not exactly, but I know she's thinking it."

"I doubt it, but I'm proud of you, bro. Going to big-boy stuff like the symphony." He fakes some sniffles and wipes a nonexistent tear from his eye. "My little boy is growing up."

"I will do anything for that guitar. Get ready to say buh-bye."

He stares at me. "The point is not the guitar. It's to be monogamous."

"Nope." I hand the pretty blonde her sandwich basket, and she gives me a bashful grin. "I'm just going through the motions, and when we part ways, I'm sure you'll hold up your end of the bargain."

Those words sound stale even to my ears. I'm only on day three with Amelia, and she's already seeping into my psyche.

"You haven't won yet, and you're supposed to be trying. You have to complete the program then show me you're still a man whore."

"I like the way I am."

He huffs. "Your loss."

I shake my head. "No, it's going to be *your* loss."

Mom drives up in her slick ride and carries the chess pies to our truck. "How are my boys doing?"

"Lots of hungry people today." I take one of the boxes from her. As we set them out in the basket next to the cash register, a thought pops into my mind. "Mom, I know you're very protective of your Benz, but I was wondering if you wouldn't mind letting me borrow it tonight."

She narrows her eyes. "What do you have in mind?"

When I describe tonight's event, Mom bounces with excitement. She not only says yes but says she'll be back after she gets it detailed. While Mom walks back to her car and punches the air with her fist, I feel Jay's stare boring into my soul.

"What?"

Jay chuckles, and I know I need to tread carefully with him and Mom and the bet. Surely, this won't blow up in my face.

For the rest of the day, Jay leaves me alone, but his words keep buzzing around in my head, which ticks me off. I see Mr. Griffin in line, so I go ahead and prepare his order so he won't have to wait long. When Mr. Griffin picks up his order, I rush out of the truck after him.

"Mr. Griffin, can I ask you a question?"

He smiles as crinkles form around his icy-blue eyes. "Do I get a free meal out of it?"

"Maybe." I clear my head and my mind. "You look like somebody who's gone to the symphony before."

"Many times."

I clear my throat. "I'm going tonight."

"Oh, a date?"

"No... just friends. It's a work thing."

He lets out a slow whistle then looks me up and down. "What are you going to wear?"

I shrug. "Jeans, I guess. I haven't thought much about it, but she said I don't have to wear a tux."

He shakes his head. "You need to put in a little more effort than that. Pfft. Young people these days. Stop by my shop on your way home, and I'll see what I can do."

My eyes brighten. "Really?"

"For a few free meals."

"Deal."

We shake, and he walks away chuckling as he eats his standard sandwich. If he can spruce me up for the occasion, I'll give him free meals for a week. This will make Amelia think I'm actually trying.

As I walk back to the truck, one of my regulars, a stunning blonde, stops me. We once met up at a club downtown. Boy, that was a night to remember.

"I do love your sandwiches."

Is she really talking about my... sandwiches? "I'm glad."

"I'll be hanging out at On the Rocks tonight. Will I see you there?"

I glance at the food truck, where Jay hangs out the window, watching. Mr. Griffin stops midbite. My gaze ping-pongs between the two men judging me, waiting to see what my next move will be. A couple of days ago, I would have dropped any plans to spend time with a woman like her, but now, I hear Amelia's terms chirping in my brain.

"Well, Sirena."

"It's Siena."

"Right. Siena. Thank you for the offer, but I'll have to pass."

She slides a hand up my chest and rests it on my shoulder with a big poofy pout. "Are you sure?"

She acts like we've been an item for months and not like we mashed on the dance floor one time. She squeezes my shoulder, trying to latch on to me. As Amelia would say, she's definitely a flea. A very gorgeous flea.

I cover her hand with mine and remove it from my body. "Yeah. I'm sure."

"If you get bored, you know where to find me." With that, she sashays off while I wonder if I just turned in my man card.

Mr. Griffin snorts and shakes his head. Jay tsks me, and on the way back toward the truck, I can't decide if I'm proud or if I should kick my own butt. Deciding I did the right thing, I throw my chest back and strut into the truck. I'm actually impressed with myself for this tiny victory. And it didn't hurt as badly as I originally thought it would.

On the other hand, if word on the street gets out that I turned down a girl like Siena, I will have to start adopting cats, which I'm sure Amelia would graciously help me out with.

The bell rings overhead as I step into Mr. Griffin's store. Circular racks of men's clothing line the middle of the shop, with built-in cubes filled with folded clothing along the walls. In the back is the register with dressing rooms on each side. When Mr. Griffin sees me, he smiles and stops arranging shirts.

"Ah, I was beginning to think you changed your mind."

"Naw, just got tied up with the daily rush." I look around at the very nice, very expensive-looking clothing. "So, go easy on me. I'm not loaded with money."

He waves me off. "This, I will do for free." He hands me some clothes hanging on a rack next to the cash register. "I took the liberty to pick out a few things I thought would be good for tonight. I also researched the concert so I could gauge what style you need."

"How do you know these will fit?"

Blankly, he stares at me. "I'm a tailor and have been doing this since before you were born. Trust me. I know what I'm doing." He jerks his head to the side. "Changing rooms are in there."

I remove my work clothes and slide into the nicest slacks I have ever touched. The dress shirt is so stiffly starched it feels like it could break in two. In my bare feet, I slide open the curtain, and Mr. Griffin grins.

"I was hoping you would try that one first. Charcoal gray is a good color for you. You almost look presentable."

I grin as I stare at what I think is my reflection in the mirror. He kneels and pins the hem of my pants, then, with creaky knees, stands. He tugs on the shirt and nods. "Just a tiny tuck here and there, and it will be perfect."

"Are you sure you don't want any money for this?"

"Just don't wear that god-awful baseball cap with this ensemble."

I grin and am a little embarrassed that I'm known for always wearing a ball cap. "I promise."

"The alterations will only take a few moments, so make yourself comfortable. Go change back into your grubby attire."

"Yes, sir."

I watch Mr. Griffin as he hems the slacks with the nimbleness of someone half his age. An old picture of a couple on their wedding day sits next to his sewing machine.

"Is that you?"

He stares at the picture, and a warm smile grows across his face. "Yes, that's me and Katarina on our wedding day. Wasn't she beautiful?"

"Yes."

He focuses on my pants. "I miss her every day. You get one shot at love like that, so embrace it with all you've got because it doesn't last forever."

"My family doesn't have a very good track record of successful relationships."

Mr. Griffin takes the pants to the pressing machine and gives them a crease down the middle. "Is that why you flirt with every girl in the park?"

"I don't... well, I like women."

"Please tell me that the one today with the puffer-fish lips isn't your date tonight."

I chuckle. "No. I, uh... it's hard to explain, but a girl is living with me for a little while."

"Oh, I didn't know you were the serious type."

"I'm not."

For the next thirty minutes, I tell Mr. Griffin all about Amelia and her side business, which makes him laugh heartily. He scowls when I admit I made a bet with Jay.

"This girl is trying to help you, and you are going to mess it all up because you want a stupid guitar?"

"It's a vintage guitar, to be more specific. Besides, I don't think I can be rehabilitated. It's not in me to settle down."

"That's a cop-out. Take it one step at a time, and tonight, enjoy the concert like a normal person. Amelia sounds lovely, and if you just be yourself, you might enjoy being with a beautiful woman who likes you for who you are."

Before I can tell Mr. Griffin that Amelia doesn't see me that way, he bags the clothing in a plastic garment bag and hands it to me. "There you go. Feel free to pick out a pair of shoes over there. You don't want to ruin this look by wearing sneakers."

My eyes bug out of my head. "Seriously? You're too kind."

"They will cost you a week's worth of meals."

"Done."

Right before I open the door to leave, he says, "Son, have fun tonight. I want to hear all about it the next time I see you."

"You got it."

I wish I could forget about the bet and that I'm Amelia's client for one night. If so, I might be able to have a great time with a beautiful girl. And no strings attached.

CHAPTER NINETEEN
Amelia

After the day I had at the shelter, I'm ready for a change of pace. I arrive home—well, back to the apartment—before Phin. I shower and dress in a strappy sundress my sister Laura helped me pick out a couple of months ago. I've been saving it for a special occasion. It has gotten folded into my luggage and toted around through two clients' homes and two stints on Dorothy's sofa. It's almost like I've been saving it for this moment.

I pull my hair into a simple French braid and am just coming out of the bathroom when I hear Phin's key in the lock.

When he sees me, he freezes in his tracks. "Wow. You look..."

Flushing, I stare down at my pretty dress and let the skirt swish around my knees. "It's not my normal canine attire, but every now and then, I look my age."

He scans me from head to toe and runs a hand through his curly hair. "You look hot."

My insides get all fluttery at his comment. It's definitely an ego boost. "That's very kind of you, but a woman likes to be called beautiful or gorgeous. Hot is reserved for..."

"For fleas?"

I nod. "See, you're learning, but I know you meant well, so I appreciate the compliment. I don't usually hear that."

He cocks his head to the side. "That's a shame because you are."

By the way he snaps his mouth closed, I think he's as surprised by his words as I am. I point to the clear plastic dry-cleaning bag. "So, whatcha got there?"

Standing tall, he smiles. "You're not the only one dressing like an adult tonight. Give me about fifteen minutes to shower and shave, and we'll head out."

While the shower is running, I finish my makeup and feed Dolly. When Phin exits the bathroom, I drop my phone. He looks good enough to eat in charcoal-gray dress slacks and one of those cool hip-bone-skimming dress shirts that doesn't need to be tucked in. The little patch of hair poking out of his neckline is my kryptonite. If he rolls up his sleeves to expose his forearms, I just might faint on the spot. These are not appropriate thoughts about a client, but I am only human.

I wipe my mouth with the back of my hand just in case drool has escaped. "You look amazing. I didn't know you had it in you."

He grins, and I think I literally swoon. "When I have to, I can GQ it up."

Yes, you can.

He juts out his elbow. "Ready to go?"

"Let's go. We can take my car. I'm not really in the mood to take the food truck or any kind of truck tonight."

He belts out a laugh. "Another adulting thing I did today was to borrow my mother's Mercedes."

My eyes grow wide. "You really are acting like a big boy tonight."

Phin rolls his eyes. "Let's go before I decide to turn on the baseball game and wear my cap."

"You will love this concert, I promise. And after, we can hang with Axel and his friends for a bit."

"Like groupies?"

"Exactly."

He holds out his hand, and I take it. It's really bad that I like how his hand feels in mine. It's warm and strong, like nothing can go wrong while he's holding on to me. He escorts me to the heavenly car, and I sink into the velvety-soft leather seats, reminding myself that I used to have a car like this, but that was before I couldn't make the payments anymore.

We drive in silence, and when we reach the auditorium, I hand him the VIP parking pass. "It sure beats looking for a parking space and waiting forever after the performance to get out of the deck. You're going to have so much fun. The timing of you being my client and this concert could not have been more perfect."

We park then weave through the crowd to our reserved seating area. Mom and Dad are already in our booth when we arrive.

"Mom, this is Phin."

Mom shakes his hand. "Nice to meet you." She then zeroes in on my injured hand. "Let me look at this." She turns my hand over and inspects the bandage. "Sweetie, why didn't you call me? I would have been there in a jiffy."

"I was in good hands, pun intended."

With a furrowed brow, she adds, "Well, it's a mother's job to worry."

I glance at Phin. "Welcome to the Day family."

Phin holds out a hand to my father, and the introductions continue. Dad pumps Phin's hand so much I feel like Phin will never be able to play the guitar again, but he takes it all in stride.

Ramona, Laura, and Dorothy stumble into the booth in a fit of giggles. When Laura sees Phin, her mouth drops. Dorothy whispers something in Ramona's ear, making her nod in agreement. Laura mouths, "Damn," as she passes us to find her seat.

Dorothy settles in next to me. "You won't believe all the things I had to promise Dax so he would watch the kids tonight."

My cringing expression makes her laugh. "I won't go into details."

"Good."

Looking up from the program, Phin asks, "Is this usually a girls-only outing?"

"My brother-in-law doesn't normally beg to go to Axel's concerts, but I guess the Beatles appeals to even the biggest heathens."

He laughs and points at the program. "They better not butcher these songs."

"I promise you'll be impressed. If you aren't, you can chop off one complete step from my program," I say.

His eyebrows raise. "Oooh. You think they are that good, huh?"

"I know they are."

The lights dim, and we settle into our seats.

I whisper in Phin's ear, "Do you see Axel down there? He doesn't look like the same guy as yesterday, right?"

Axel walks on stage wearing black slacks and a long-sleeve black dress shirt and has his hair pulled back in a ponytail.

Phin smiles. "Not at all."

When they start the performance, I sneak a peek at Phin. He leans forward, propping his elbows on his thighs as his laser focus stays on the performers. The music flows around us, from "Penny Lane" to "Eleanor Rigby." It wraps us in its familiarity and takes our breath away with the beauty of the notes rising and falling. At one point, Phin closes his eyes, and knowing how my brother is, Phin must be feeling the notes deep in his soul. He is loving this. He hasn't fidgeted. He hasn't excused himself for the bathroom.

They roll into "Let it Be," leading into the finale. He scrubs his face with his hands and pumps a fist in the air to the beat. I pat his thigh, and without losing a beat, he takes my uninjured hand in his, lacing his fingers with mine, and squeezes it.

My heart hammers in my chest, drowning out the music. His thumb rubs the back of my hand, and I forget how to breathe. When he turns to me, our eyes meet, and he winks. I blush and have to look away. Hobby events are good for the client. They are a point in the process when the man either shows me who he can become or proves that he's a waste of my time. It's all about the client. It's not supposed to make my heart do whatever it's doing inside my chest, because it's not about me. This is supposed to change him, not me.

Yet, here I am, with warm bubbles popping in my bloodstream all the way down to my toes. I haven't felt like this in years—like I was dormant and now am alive. I release a breath and rest my head on his shoulder. He turns and kisses my forehead, and I am officially a goner.

He whispers, "Thank you."

I hope he doesn't hear me sigh.

When the last song is over, Phin stands and claps so loudly I think Axel will hear him from the stage. Phin is having the time of his life. He turns to me. "I'm hooked."

I think he just turned a corner. I hope I can let him go when the time comes.

CHAPTER TWENTY

Phin

I went to my first concert when I was thirteen, and I felt then how I feel now. My heart is racing, and the muscles in my face are set to a perpetual smile. I'm blown away by the melding of all the instruments into one large sound. *How have I missed out on this?* When they played "In My Life," I almost lost it. I could almost hear my mother's voice from when I was young overlaying with the notes. I coughed into my hand so Amelia wouldn't see how much it affected me. My eyes definitely misted.

The stage musicians have finished the encore, and the crowd around us, including Amelia's family, starts moving toward the exits, but I can't move. I am not ready for this feeling to end.

What will Amelia make of my take on the concert? If she can't sense it by the way I took her hand in mine and even kissed her forehead, I don't know what else could be more telling. I was overwhelmed with pure joy so much that I let my guard down, and it felt amazing.

Her family leaves us to meet with Axel. Other than a few stragglers, we are mostly alone in the row. I'm in no hurry to leave this happy bubble, and Amelia doesn't push me out into the aisle.

While we stand there, staring at each other, she asks, "So, what did you think?"

"I don't have the words."

"Life changing, huh?"

"Definitely." I slide my hand to her soft neck and whisper in her ear, "Thank you. I know it was only a part of the steps, but I'll never forget this."

She blushes. "I figured, since you're a musician, you'd get a kick out of it."

"I loved every minute of it, but... it wasn't just the music."

Did I just say that out loud? I may have crossed a professional line with her, but I can't help speaking the truth. For once, it's not a silly pickup line. I mean it, even as the words spill from my mouth. She made tonight special.

She bows her head then jerks it toward the exit. "Come on, let's catch up to my family and congratulate Axel."

When we arrive backstage, Amelia's sisters already surround their brother. Her dad snaps pictures on his cell phone of him and his mother. Axel's face glistens with sweat. His hair is down out of the ponytail he had during the concert, and he's already untucked his shirt, looking more like the Axel I first met.

Amelia hugs him, and I almost break his hand I shake it so hard.

"Man, that was awesome. I didn't expect that at all," I say.

He grins, and I see the family resemblance. He has the same crooked smile as Amelia and even has freckles over his nose like she does.

"Thanks. I love doing tribute concerts. The crowd really gets into them."

"I think I'm going to buy season tickets. That was unbelievable."

"No need. If you keep hanging with my sis, you can always have a ticket."

Amelia clears her throat and glares at him. "You know the rules."

Axel throws his hands up in defense. "I know, but come on. He's a music lover."

She wags her finger at her brother, and he growls.

The thought of spending time with Amelia after our contract is over isn't as scary as it might have been only a few days ago. Before I can interject my opinion, Amelia's dad corrals the family around Axel for a photo.

"Why don't you let me take the picture so you can be in it too?" I hold out my hand to take his phone.

Her dad hands me his phone, and I take several shots. For one, they smile proudly, but the next, they all point, each one in a different direction. I'm assuming that's a Day tradition.

I give the phone back to Mr. Day, and he scrunches me next to Amelia. She glances up at me, and I squeeze her shoulders right as the camera flash goes off.

"Dad, take another one. I wasn't looking."

They take several more and even one with my phone because I never want to forget this moment.

Axel looks at his gaggle of sisters. "Who's up for pie?"

"Me!" they yell at the same time.

As if reading my mind, Amelia says, "We always go to Three Point One Four after the concerts to celebrate."

"Clever. I could go for pie."

She bounces up and down, clapping like I just made her day, when it's the other way around. I am at a loss for words the entire walk to the shop. Lost in my thoughts, I hang back a little to watch the Day family as they cut up with one another. Amelia walks backward and motions for me to catch up, so I jog to meet her. She hip bumps me, and I give her one back, something I have *never* done in my entire life.

What is wrong with me?

When I walk through the door, the smells of fruit, sugar, and cinnamon waft over me, making my eyes roll back into my head. "Why haven't I been here before?"

"Beats me. It's only the coolest place in town." Amelia hands me a menu that lists at least twenty varieties of pie. "This has been a tradition ever since Axel was little. Every time he would have a recital, we'd celebrate here. I think he'd retire from music if this place closed."

"I heard that," Axel says.

Mr. Day pops his son on the back. "Son, you're too good to give it up. Even if you quit the cello, there's always the violin, the French horn, guitar..."

My ears perk up. "You still play the guitar?"

"Bass guitar, mostly. When I was little, my dad got me backstage at a Wings concert, and I met Paul McCartney. I've been hooked ever since."

I whisper in Amelia's ear, "I think I've found my soulmate."

She belts out a laugh and bops me on the head with the menu. "Order, then you can fanboy all you want."

She winks, and I have the strangest urge to hug her.

"I plan on it."

As I peruse the menu, I can't help but notice all the love that surrounds Amelia's family. They tease and care for each other constantly. Growing up, it was only me and Mom, and she worked so hard all the time. When she was at home, she was dog-tired. But the two things we shared a love for were food and music. We didn't have much more than that, but it was always enough. When my long-lost dad passed away, at least he did the decent thing to leave a life insurance policy in my mother's name so she never had to stress about money again.

"Have you decided?" Amelia's question breaks my train of thought.

"It's a toss-up between the apple and the key lime pie."

Amelia gives me a thumbs-up. "Oooh, both are very good. How about you order the apple and I get the key lime and we share?"

I slap my menu on the counter. "Deal. I like how you think."

As we sit at a large table in the back, everyone chows down. Amelia takes a bite of hers then a bite of mine, and strangely, I don't care. Axel sits on the other side of me, inhaling his chocolate cream pie.

When Amelia leaves the table to go to the restroom, Axel says, "So, you and my sister..."

"I'm her client."

"Yeah, I hear ya. At least you're helping her pay off the mountain of debt that jackass Bennet left her with."

"Yeah? What's the story there?"

"They were on the way to the altar, and he got cold feet, thank God. During their time together, she did her best to keep up with his friends."

My eyes grow wide, and I stop eating.

"Yup. Jet-setting around every month, expensive cars, jewelry, you name it. She did it to hobnob with that obnoxious crowd, and that tightwad didn't help her out at all. He walked away, even though he makes six figures, and left her with all the debt. If you couldn't tell, I can't stand the jackass."

I am floored to think of somebody jilting Amelia at the altar. She's practically perfect. If that Bennet ever comes by the food truck and I know who he is, I might just beat the crap out of him for her.

He sighs. "I worry about her. She didn't even give herself enough time to be mad or hurt, and now she focuses on making others happy. I don't think she knows how to find happiness."

"Wow. I mean, why would someone hurt her? Nothing's wrong with her."

Axel snorts.

"Except for the fact that she's perpetually happy."

"It's a mask she wears."

I scrub my face. "Why are you telling me this?"

He wipes a crumb from his beard. "Because I want my sister to be happy, and the way you two look together..."

"We're not together-together."

Axel rolls his eyes. "Whatever, dude."

I clear my throat. "So, my business partner and I like to jam occasionally. Want to join us sometime?"

His eyes light up. "Absolutely."

While I tell him about Jay's guitar, which has Axel twitching in his seat, Amelia plunks down beside me again. "Are you going to eat that last bite?"

I load my fork with the apple pie and feed it to her.

She closes her eyes and moans. "Best ever."

Axel chuckles.

"What's so funny?" she asks her brother.

All of her family stop chattering to stare at Axel. He clears his throat and buries his head as he stares at his pie like it's the most interesting thing on the planet. "Nothing."

She sneers. "Axel, why didn't you invite Liberty to the concert? You know how much she loves to watch you play."

"Yeah, son," their mother chimes in. "I just adore her."

Axel squirms as his entire family waits for his answer. He stuffs his mouth full of pie.

I would recognize that uncomfortable posturing from a mile away. "Maybe she was busy."

The youngest sister—I think her name is Laura—shakes her head. "Nope. I talked to her this morning, and I think you hurt her feelings when you didn't invite her."

He sets the fork down and cocks his head. "We're not together."

A smile spreads across my face, and I know I shouldn't say it, but I can't pass up the opportunity. "Do you mean together-together?"

"You suck."

In my mind, I relive every moment of the evening as we drive back to my apartment. Amelia's mouth opens in a big yawn, and what would normally irritate the crap out of me makes me grin.

"Tired?"

"Yeah. Work was crazy today, and sitting still for an entire concert was difficult."

"I thought I heard you snoring."

She snorts. "I did not."

"Did too, and right when they were playing 'Penny Lane' of all songs. Have you no shame?"

Amelia smiles as she stares out the window, her injured hand propped on the door. "Did you enjoy the concert?"

"Enjoy? That's an understatement. It was amazing."

"I noticed you and Axel getting along nicely."

I nod. "He's really cool. How he survives being surrounded by that much estrogen is beyond me."

She playfully pops me on the shoulder. "He manages just fine and knows how to handle it. Having a gaggle of sisters is good training for him."

I scratch the back of my neck. The dress collar is starting to constrict my breathing. "We might get together and jam sometime soon."

She shakes her head. "Nope. He knows better."

"He knows better than to what?"

Amelia pulls out her phone, and her thumbs fly over the screen in a frenzy. "He knows better than to befriend my clients. He's supposed to be nice but not get friendly."

"That's stupid. Why not? We have similar hobbies—or in his case, it's more than just a hobby, and I'm a bit envious about that part, but you know what I mean. If I had met him without this crazy arrangement, we still would have clicked, and you know it."

She reads her screen and lets out a groan before slamming her phone back into her purse. "Agh. I know, but it's just that he shouldn't get attached, because after our business relationship is complete, we may never see each other again, and I don't make a habit of intruding on my clients' lives after they find their true loves."

I snap my finger. "I get it. He has kennel cough."

She bites her lip to keep from laughing. "Oh, hush. It just gets messy if our personal and professional lives get entangled."

I guess she always rests her head on her clients' shoulders and invites them to eat pie with her family. For a moment, I thought we shared something more than what was contractual, but I guess not.

"Right. No long-term connections. Got it." Just when she was starting to worm her way into my heart, like she wormed her way into my apartment, she puts me in my place.

I pull into the parking lot and jump out of the driver's seat, slamming the door behind me. I do the gentlemanly thing by opening her car door, but then I storm toward my apartment without her by my side.

"Are you mad at me?"

Her soft voice behind me causes me to pause and release a sigh. "No. You're right. This is a business arrangement. But tonight, it felt like, well... it was really nice."

I open the door and allow her to enter first. A trail of perfume wafts past me. Forcing myself to avoid taking a deep whiff, I hold my breath as I enter behind her.

"I thought so too. You just passed a big hurdle in our contract. One more poodle piece removed from the board."

I fight to not roll my eyes.

She stares off, and after a second, she blows out a breath and adds with a shaky voice, "Before you know it, I'll be out of your hair and out of your apartment. Keep this up, and you'll be done with me sooner than you think, and you'll never have to see me again."

That's what I'm afraid of.

CHAPTER TWENTY-ONE
Amelia

Journal Entry 4

There have been several setbacks already with this client, first the poker game (which was a complete ploy to get me to back out of the contract) and also my injury, but Phin Baxtor has made great progress even so. The plan is moving forward, and the hobby event was better than I imagined.

Axel's concert could not have been more perfect for this client. Phin was completely into it and blended well with the family. The standard meet and greet may not be necessary with this client, as I was able to combine two steps into one event.

If this client continues on this path, he will have completed my system in record time. On a personal note, I'm not sure how I feel about leaving Phin. More than my brother, I'm starting to forget he's a client and not a friend, or more.

Note to self:

Start the search for the next client immediately.

Discipline Axel for getting too close to my client.

Discipline myself for getting too close to my client as well.

My phone chirps, waking me and notifying me of a text message.

Axel: *Thanks for being there last night.*

Grrr. He knows better than to interact any more than superficially with my clients. I text him back.

Me: *You crossed a line, buddy.*

Axel: *Me???*

Me: *Yes, you. Don't get close to Phin.*

Axel: [Eyeroll emoji] *Why?*

Me: *Because I don't want you to get too attached. He's my client, re-member?*

Axel: *Just a client... Sure.*

Me: *Yes.*

Axel: *I saw the way he looked at you last night. No guy has ever drunk you in like that, not even the asshat, Bennet.*

Truth be told, I did notice how Phin couldn't keep his eyes and hands off me. Every chance he got, his hands found my shoulder or waist, and it wasn't to cop a feel either. It was much more intimate than that, and I should kick myself for enjoying it so much. In fact, instead of sending negative vibes with each brush of his hand, I would lean into his touch, each one sending a host of butterflies scurrying around my stomach. And revisiting the night makes me all gushy inside. *This is so bad.*

Me: *We don't use the B word anymore.*

Axel: *Sorry. Phin is different, and in case you didn't notice, you're not my boss. If I want to jam with a fellow music lover, I will. In fact, I might tell him I caught you kissing your Bon Jovi poster when you were fifteen.*

I suck in a huge breath. *Harsh.*

Me: *A good brother wouldn't do that. I have to go. And go back to sleep. It's way too early for a musician to be awake.*

Axel sends me a bunch of laughing smiley face emojis, which ticks me off, so I reply one last time.

Me: *From my seat last night, I had a good view of that bald spot on the top of your head.*

That'll shut him up, at least for the rest of the day. Any other time, I think he and Phin could be great friends, but I have to keep my family from getting too attached to my clients. It has a chance to get very messy otherwise. Up until now, it hasn't been an issue. I should examine the difference with Phin and my family, but right now, I don't want to dive too deeply into that for fear of what I might find out about myself.

The scent of coffee tickles my nose, and even though I got zero sleep, it wakes me completely. I roll off my blow-up mattress and land on the floor with a thud, making Dolly jump up and shake.

"Sorry, girl. Let's take you outside."

I give her a scratch under the chin and leave the confines of my room in search of coffee. Before I get halfway down the hall, I hear a woman's voice. If Phin hooked up with someone last night after the progress he's made, I might have to smack him into next week. I screech to a halt, bump into the wall, and backpedal, but Phin appears a moment later.

"You're awake. I want you to meet someone."

"You have company?" I screech.

Realizing I'm in a skimpy tank top and very short shorts, I scurry back into my room and slam the door, toss on some sweats, and throw a T-shirt over my head then blow the hair out of my face. After I take a few deep breaths to settle my nerves and hash out what I need to say to my client, I turn the knob to open my bedroom door. When I enter the kitchen, the long head-to-toe gaze Phin gives me makes me glad I threw on some clothes.

"Hi."

No other syllables spill from my mouth as Dolly makes a beeline for Phin, insisting he pet her. He scratches her head and is rewarded with a kiss on the hand.

A lovely woman in about her late forties who has the same curly brown hair and broad smile as Phin extends her hand for me to shake. I accept it, and her hand is as warm and inviting as her smile.

"So very nice to meet you. I'm Vivian, Phin's mom. I heard you had a wonderful time last night. He can't stop talking about it."

Our eyes meet, and he shrugs while he sips on his coffee. "She Ubered here to get her car."

I look down at my sloppy attire. "I'm sorry I'm so underdressed. I smelled coffee, and my brain cells won't fire right until they have been properly lubricated. This is Dolly, my dog."

She leans down and lets Dolly lick her face. I like this woman already.

Phin chuckles. "Don't let her fool you. Her normal dress code isn't much better."

My jaw drops. "I'll have you know I dress properly for work."

"True, and at least you covered those sexy legs."

His eyes grow big, then he clears his throat as his mother quirks an eyebrow.

"I mean, they would get all scratched up." He glances at his mother and adds, "She works with animals, and she usually has a layer of dog hair everywhere."

He holds out a mug of coffee for me, and I snatch it out of his hand.

"As opposed to you, who wears band T-shirts splattered with mustard and grease," I say.

His mom laughs. "I like her already."

I stick out my tongue at Phin, and he rolls his eyes, but his mouth twitches like he's trying not to smile.

"Don't get attached. It's a business arrangement, remember?" he says to his mom.

"Oh, yes. Amelia, I think your consulting business is brilliant."

He stares at the ceiling. "Mom."

"Seriously. Take my son here. He's a great guy and very handsome, if I do say so myself, but he doesn't know the first thing about relationships."

"Oh God," he mumbles.

Vivian shakes her head. "It's not his fault. He didn't have a male role model to emulate."

"She doesn't want to know—"

I hold up a hand to stop him. "I would love to know more. Backstory is key to future success."

Phin's neck gets all splotchy as he puts an arm around her shoulders. "Another time, Mom. Let's get to work." He eyes me. "Have a nice day, Amelia."

Grinning, I say, "Actually, I'm off today. I planned to observe you at work. If you read the schedule, you would know that."

"There's a schedule?"

I give him a warning glance as I continue. "It's part of the natural-habitat portion of my system. It's important I see the man's place of business to determine if he's a proper breadwinner. He can't be playing guitar in a bar for the rest of his life." With a wink, I let Phin know I am only kidding—mostly.

"You've already seen me at work."

I shrug one shoulder. "True, but besting you at trivia isn't quite the same thing."

There goes that muscle twitch in his jaw again, but this time, he adds the cutest twinkle in his eyes.

Vivian claps her hands. "I have a great idea."

"Oh no." He leans over to whisper in my ear, "Her ideas usually involve me carrying something heavy."

She swats at her son. "The park is having a huge festival today with lots of customers, so I'm helping Phin and Jay in the truck. Since you're going to be there anyway, do you want to help us? Every extra hand would be useful."

That sounds like as much fun as getting a root canal, but meeting his family is on my to-do list. And since Vivian is the only family he has, it would be the perfect way to plow through the contract. Plus, I would get to spend time with a really cool lady.

He cringes. "Amelia, why don't we skip that step? It's not a good day for it."

I shake my head. "It's nonnegotiable. And meeting your family is necessary, so I'll be there, ready to observe and help."

Vivian claps like a cheerleader, but Phin groans as he ushers her outside. He turns around. "You might want to do something with that hair, or you'll scare all the customers away."

I fake like I'm going to hit him, and he scurries outside, with me and Dolly right behind him.

"Come on, Dolly. Do your business so I can get ready to work on my day off."

While I wait on Dolly to find the perfect spot to pee, Phin helps his mother into her car. When he gets in the food truck, I hear the engine turn over, and he toots the horn as he exits the parking lot.

I let out a groan. "Time to get presentable." To Dolly, I ask, "I don't look *that* bad, do I?"

She growls at me, so I take that as a yes.

CHAPTER TWENTY-TWO
Phin

Every food truck in the city lines up at one end of the park to prepare for the big event. The booths in rows come to life with every craft known to man, while techs prepare the sound system for what will be live music and a makeshift dance floor later in the day. The artisan festival draws a large crowd and will be busy from sunup to sundown, but the profits will be worth it. While Jay and I set up the truck, Mom pulls out the whiteboard and adds today's specials.

As she busies herself outside, Jay clears his throat. "How did your *date* go last night?"

Gritting my teeth, I focus on chopping tomatoes. "It wasn't a *date*. Truth be told, the concert blew me away. So even with having to dress up a bit, it was not horrible." My lip quirks up into a smile, and I work my jaw to keep Jay from seeing it.

He closes the cash register and chuckles. "I told you she was a miracle worker."

"Shh. Mom knows about Amelia and her consulting business, but I'm sure she thinks there's more than just a business arrangement."

"Is there?"

I glare at Jay, daring him to say anything else. "Not a word to Mom about our bet. Got it?"

"My lips are sealed."

Girly laughter outside the truck catches our attention.

Jay's eyes grow big as he looks over my shoulder. "I think you might be right."

He motions with his head, and when I turn to see Mom and Amelia laughing about something, my stomach does a flip-flop. Amelia has her hair in a ponytail and pulled through the loop of a baseball cap. Her shorts reveal muscular legs that make my mouth go dry.

As if she can feel my stare, she turns to me and grins while she does a girly finger wave. And she brought her dog, who decides to take up residence under the truck in the shade.

I hang out the window of the food truck and watch Amelia skip toward me. The girl frickin' skips, and I find it hard to pull my eyes away from her childish mannerisms.

She grins up at me. "Hey, boss. What would you like me to do?"

Stop being so cute, that's what. Lost in my thoughts, I don't answer her.

"Phin? Are you okay?"

I blink a few times before realizing I zoned out. "Yeah, the festival is going to be crazy busy, so if you would like to take orders on one of these order pads before they get to the front of the line, that would speed things up."

"Got it." She takes a pad from my hand as my fingers graze her injured palm.

"And no giving out trivia."

She snaps her fingers. "Darn. I was going to get each one to stump you today."

"If you do, I will go broke. You don't want that, do you?"

"Just kidding, kind of." Amelia singsongs her words.

Mom whistles, making me jump so high I hit my head on the overhead bin. "Ow."

We both watch Amelia saunter away, when Mom says, "Honey, I know you are her client, but..."

"But nothing. Let's get this day started."

Mom shakes her head. Jay holds up his hands as if to say, *Don't look at me,* as customers start lining up. With Amelia keeping the customers entertained in line and Mom helping with filling the orders, we have a nice, smooth system going. When Amelia's caught up with the line, she helps Mom hand out orders. She's like a human Energizer Bunny.

As we work through the lunch crowd, Amelia seems to have more energy instead of less, and a couple of times, she catches me staring at her. Sometimes, she crosses her eyes, making me shake my head with laughter.

The crowd dwindles, and while I clean up the condiment mess I made, Amelia yells, "Oh no, you don't!"

Her brother, Axel, stands next to her, holding the hand of a very pretty lady about Amelia's age. Amelia crosses her arms over her chest and shakes her head. The girl on Axel's arm says something to Amelia, making her shoulders slump. She then waves them toward the truck.

"'Sup, Phin."

"I take it you got a tongue-lashing from your sister."

He rolls his eyes then glances over his shoulder to where Amelia and the lady chat. "It wasn't my idea to come here. Women love art festivals."

Jay chuckles. "You better fill your stomach because you're gonna need all the sustenance you can get."

Axel whimpers. "Are we still going to jam?"

Before I can answer, Jay shouts, "Hell yeah!"

"Shh," I say. "If Amelia hears us, I'll get put in time-out."

Axel belts out a laugh. "We are in the cone of silence."

As he leaves, I say to Jay, "I hope he doesn't know about our trivia free-meal deal."

"*Our* cone of silence, buddy."

During a lull in the crowd, we sit outside the truck, catching our breath and slurping down water. Jay plays his guitar almost as if he's teasing me and trying to remind me of what's on the line. Amelia sits cross-legged in the grass, searching for something while Dolly lays on her back like a dead roach.

When Amelia finds a four-leaf clover, she plucks it up and hands it to me. "For you."

"I don't need luck."

Mom rolls her eyes. "We all need a little luck every now and then. Or fate, or whatever it's called. Sometimes, things happen. People come into your life without any rhyme or reason, and you just need to go with the flow."

I stare up at the sky. Someone, just shoot me here and now because I know where she's headed with this. Standing up, I turn my baseball cap to its proper position and walk away.

"Where are you going?" Mom asks.

"Anywhere that isn't here."

Mom laughs. "Amelia, why don't you and Phin take a break and go visit the booths? Jay and I have this."

I stare down at Amelia, who has gone ghostly white. The wheels in her head turn as she nods to herself. "Okay. I think that sounds like fun." She looks down at Dolly. "You stay at the truck. Jay, don't feed her French fries no matter how much she begs. Trust me, it's not a pretty sight later."

Jay laughs as he scratches Dolly's belly. "Got it."

Amelia stands, dusts off her shorts, and catches up to me. We walk in silence past the face-painting booth and the dream catcher table. I stop to check out the handmade scarves. My mom would love the purple one.

"Your mom means well, but look at it this way. We're checking off another item on the list. We are out on the town to see how you handle girls hitting on you."

I scoff. "Girls don't hit on guys at craft fairs."

She waves a hand in front of us like a model on *The Price is Right*. "Blond girl at twelve o'clock. She is pretending to focus on the watercolor paintings, but she has not taken her eyes off you."

That would be Jill. We had fun about a month ago. The business card with her name on it is definitely crumpled.

Amelia looks over her shoulder. "Tall brunette behind us has been following you ever since we left the truck. By the way, she asked if you had any vegan peanut butter." She rolls her eyes.

Glancing over my shoulder, I do my best to see who she's talking about without being obvious, and damn, like I remember, Vanessa is a looker. I smile then turn back around. "No big deal."

"Okay, let's see what happens."

Amelia trots away, finds a random dude, and pulls him onto the dance floor. While they boogie to an awful cover band, Vanessa slinks up to me. Her perfume is suffocatingly strong. "I'm hoping that's your sister."

"Not hardly."

Another guy takes Amelia by the hand, swinging her around, and she giggles as he takes her in his arms. Her smile broadens, if that's even possible.

"Want to dance?" Vanessa asks, snapping me out of my fog.

I turn to take in the beauty standing next to me then glance back at Amelia, who is now doing a two-step with yet a third guy. The two women couldn't be more different. Before I met Amelia, I would have given Vanessa a second glance, but today, I'm totally off my game. *Damn you, Amelia Day.*

"I'm good, but thanks for the offer."

She huffs as I walk toward Amelia. Her laughter is infectious. When she sees me, her smile lights up her face. "Hey."

I hold out my hand. "Come on, Shakira. We better get back to work."

She waves to the guys she was dancing with as she walks next to me. We pass Vanessa.

Amelia waves at her. "Did you get her number?"

"Nope." *I already have her number but don't really care.*

Her mouth drops open. "Really? Why not?"

I slide my arm around Amelia's neck and mess with her baseball cap. "I was a little distracted by your dance skills. Better than your singing, that's for sure."

She squeezes me around my waist. "Aww. I'm so proud of you. You easily could have taken her home, and you didn't. See? You're getting better at weeding out the fleas."

I stare at her, then it hits me what she means. It's another one of her dog metaphors. Vanessa is gorgeous but would have been a flea that I wouldn't want around more than a day.

I'm not sure if I should thank Amelia for helping me figure that out or be angry because girls like the brown-haired beauty are so much fun. But in the long run, they are hard to get rid of. Maybe Amelia's techniques have some merit, but I would never let her know that.

CHAPTER TWENTY-THREE
Amelia

No offense to Dolly, but I am dog-tired after working at the festival all day. I have sweat stains under my arms and down my back, and I may never get the mustard stain off my favorite "I don't care what happens in the movie as long as the dog lives" T-shirt. Thank goodness my injury isn't so painful today, or I would have been a mess trying to do everything with one hand. I had such a great time, even though I almost fell asleep at a traffic light on the way back to the apartment.

Phin is cruising through the steps. The way he turned down that flea of a woman is a turning point. It won't be long now until my work here is done, and I am not sure I'm ready to go. I don't normally feel a pull toward my clients, and it's unnerving how I wish Phin wasn't one. I enjoy my time with him more than I should, and it doesn't matter what we're doing—going to a concert, cleaning the apartment, a trip to urgent care. Even today, working my butt off was amazing because it was with him. And that is what I hope my clients feel as well. Marriage isn't about the big events. It's all about the tiny things.

I sit in my parking space, rolling out my sore neck muscles, when Dolly decides it's time for a walk. While she sniffs around, Phin pulls up in the food truck. When she sees him jump out, she wags her tail so much I think it's going to fall off.

He kneels and claps his hands. To Dolly, he says, "Come here, girl. You know you want to."

Dolly kicks her back legs then takes off toward him, yanking the leash out of my grip. She does a full-body wag when he scratches her chin. As he scoops her up, he leans his face away to avoid Dolly's affections, and I have to shake my head to dismantle the thoughts going through my mind. Nothing is sexier than a big, strong man holding a tiny dog. And to think he didn't like her just a few days ago.

After receiving one more lick attempt, he says, "Come on, fleabag. Let's get you inside. You can tell me how much you liked working with me today, and I'll tell you about this flea I met."

I belt a laugh as I hold out my hands to retrieve my dog.

He turns his back on me. "Nope. We have lots to discuss."

Following him into the apartment, I say, "I thought you didn't like dogs."

"I don't, but I'm trying to be nice and open-minded." He grimaces when Dolly's tongue contacts his nose. Phin bends to place her back on the ground, and she circles his feet while we enter the apartment. "So, how did you think today went?" he asks with slight hesitation.

From the kitchen, he pulls out two bottles of water and hands one to me.

"Very well. I was able to cross several milestones off your list. I observed you working. I met your mother, and you used good judgment on the women swimming around you."

Phin plops down on the couch and pats the cushion next to him, convincing Dolly to jump up to sit beside him. I slide into the chair and gape at how Dolly has charmed Phin in less than a week.

"The night is young. What else can we cross off your scruffy-dog list? I'm on a roll and wouldn't want to mess anything up." He cheeses at me as Dolly circles three times then settles in next to him with a sigh.

"What about playtime?"

His eyebrows raise as his water bottle stops midway to his mouth. "Excuse me?"

I cringe. "Besides *that*, what is your favorite recreational thing you like to do?"

Phin whispers in Dolly's ear, "She has not been paying attention." He motions with his head toward the guitars hanging on the wall.

"Of course. That's perfect. Teach me to play a song on your guitar."

He stands, retrieves one of the guitars, and slides the strap over my shoulder. His hand grazes my arm as he adjusts the instrument. "We need to sit close so I can help you with where to put your hands. You can't really hit the chords with that bandage."

Sit close? You don't have to tell me twice.

I collapse onto the couch, and he sinks down right behind me, his breath tickling my neck. He puts his left hand on the neck of the guitar and slides his right arm around me, clasping my right hand in his. Positioning the fingers on my trembling right hand on the strings, he helps me strum a note. I'm sure cats run scared all over the county.

"That was a D chord."

I strum on my own while he slides his right hand down my back and rests it on my waist. My strumming stops because it is completely impossible to focus on playing a guitar with his warm hand on my body.

"Try it again."

"Oh yeah."

He moves his strong fingers on his left hand, making the muscles in his forearm pop. *Who cares about making music right now?* I just want to gawk.

With his arms wrapped around me, he strums the guitar with ease. "See? Easy."

Staring at the guitar and his strong hands picking at the strings, I finally find my words. "What did we just play?"

"I'm hurt you didn't know it. What was the mayor of Liverpool's declaration on August 30, 1999?"

I shrug. "I'm guessing it has something to do with the Beatles."

He plays the chords again, and it hits me.

"Oh. 'Yellow Submarine.'"

"Good job. It's probably the easiest Beatles song to learn to play." With his arms still around me, he plays the song and sings the silly lyrics.

I place my hands over his to get the feel of strumming, and he stops midsong.

"Want to learn anything else?"

That's a loaded question, and I need to glue my mouth shut before I reply.

I jump off the couch and shove the guitar in his face. "I think that's enough for one night." Pretending my hand hurts, I add, "My cut is starting to throb."

With concern on his face, he takes my hand in his. "I forgot about that. I'm sorry."

"It's fine." I snatch my hand out of his hold.

No more touching! Gah. Things were going great, then we had to get *too* playful during playtime. This hasn't happened with any of my other clients, so I'm at a loss for how to pull back into the professional lane.

I turn my back and march to the bathroom to splash water on my face with my good hand. I fume at myself for feeling a hint of attraction to him. Staring at the mirror, I talk to myself. "He's a client. He's not interested in me, and he shouldn't be anyway."

When I exit the bathroom, Phin stands there holding Dolly. In a soft voice, without making eye contact, he says, "Dolly's ready for bed now."

As I take her, his hand brushes against mine, and I do my best to ignore the warmth.

More touching. Stop. No, don't stop. "Thanks. You didn't have to do that. It's not part of the contract."

He smiles, but it doesn't reach his eyes. "It's no problem. Good night, Amelia."

"Night."

Right before he reaches his bedroom door, he turns back to me. "And thanks for today. You were a big help, and I had fun. I can't remember the last time I enjoyed myself with a woman other than my mother without her expecting anything from me."

Knife straight to the heart. I salute him and swallow the stupid girlish crush. "Just doing my job."

"Right," he says with a husky chuckle.

It will be another long night with that man sleeping across the hall from me, especially since he's just going through the motions of what he has to do to complete the contract. This should make me happy, and in the morning, I need to start focusing on finding my next client. That's the only way to keep everything professional between us. Before long, I won't have to see him daily.

I snuggle Dolly and whisper, "Don't get too attached. You're worse than Axel."

Dolly kisses my nose as I carry her to my room and settle onto the blow-up mattress for another night of tossing and turning.

My head barely hits the pillow, when my phone starts blowing up with messages. Knowing I should just ignore them, I turn my phone to see what all the hubbub is about.

Laura: *OMG*

Dorothy: *No frickin' way. Are you ok?*

Axel: *Want me to beat him up?*

Ramona: *He didn't deserve you anyway.*

Hazel: *Don't check your social media page.*

Well, that's a surefire way to get me to pull it up. Rolling over on the mattress, I open the app, and Hazel was right. I should not have looked. That jerk Bennet had the nerve to tag me on his engagement announcement, and my heart sinks into my stomach. Engaged. *The man who said he wasn't marriage material and left me with a mountain of debt is getting married?*

Dolly must sense my mood, because she crawls up into my lap while I scroll through the comments. Through blurred vision from copious amounts of tears, I read each one.

You two are perfect for each other.

I knew she was the one!

Gorgeous couple.

Gah! I can't read any more. We were supposed to be perfect for each other. At least, that's what I thought, but he left me at the altar *and* with a mountain of debt for trying to "hang with the cool kids." I never fit in with his upper-crust crowd, but I was willing to do anything to prove to Bennet that I fit in and assumed he would help pay the bills once we got married. I rock back and forth, doing my best to breathe without crying out loud because the last thing I want to do is let Phin know what's going on.

Wiping the tears off my cheeks, I leash Dolly, grab my purse and phone, and tiptoe down the hallway and out of Phin's apartment. I can't stay here tonight. I need to go somewhere safe to do a massive ugly cry.

To my sister's house I go after I send her a text that I'm heading her way and another to Phin.

Me: *Something has come up. I need to put the contract on pause for a few days. Will contact you soon.*

Hopefully, he won't read the text until I'm long gone. I just can't face him right now, and I might not ever be able to.

CHAPTER TWENTY-FOUR
Phin

Jay side-eyes me as I slam another sandwich together. My mind spins with what went wrong, and I'm not being polite to my customers. When I woke up this morning, Amelia was already gone. I thought we were doing great. Her family was funny. The concert was off the charts, and she said I was doing amazing with the steps. Hell, I even voluntarily passed up hooking up with Vanessa. Maybe I got too touchy-feely with our guitar lesson and that freaked her out.

"What's the matter?" Jay counts some change and gives it to the customer. "You've been ornerier than a neutered bull today."

I will not admit to Jay that the apartment was uncomfortably quiet without Amelia's presence. He would never let me hear the end of it if I did.

"Dude, I think she might have backed out on the contract. You may need to kiss that guitar goodbye." I dive into making Mr. Griffin's order.

"What's that supposed to mean?"

I rub my face with my hands. "I don't know, man. She sent me a text last night to say she had to put the contract on hold to take care of some personal stuff." I roll my eyes as if it makes no difference to me.

"That doesn't sound like the Amelia I know. Did you try to call her?" Jay gives the next customer the receipt and slides the order my way on the wire.

"No. If she wanted to talk to me, she would have called." I wrack my brain, trying to figure out what I did wrong. She did call it a night shortly after our guitar lesson, but I thought we were doing good, getting along well. She didn't seem upset, only said her hand hurt.

Mr. Griffin huffs as he inspects his usual order. "You don't know the first thing about women. How did the concert go, or should I not ask?"

"It was fine." I let out a huge groan. "I'm sorry, Mr. Griffin. It was amazing. Amelia was impressed with my—or rather, *your*—clothes."

He grins. "I do know clothes."

"I'll bring them back to you as soon as I get them dry-cleaned."

He waves me off. "Nah. Keep them. You actually cleaned up nicely."

"Too good," I mumble.

"Maybe you'll have another use for them when you ask *her* out."

The thought of asking Amelia out on a date that has nothing to do with the business arrangement sends my heart racing as well as a shiver down my spine. She would never go out with me, mainly because I'm her client, but most importantly, it's obvious I would only hurt her in the end.

"I don't think that's going to happen anytime soon."

"That's too bad, but thanks for the free sandwich."

"I think you should call her anyway." Typical Jay won't leave it alone.

"Nope."

"Why? What's wrong?"

"I'm what is wrong. I'm incorrigible." I force a smile that I know he doesn't buy, because he looks like he could cry. I turn my attention to the next order as my mind sizzles with different scenarios.

"Oh... *her*. Is it her or her methods?"

"Her methods, her personality, her dog. It's everything. And I don't know how much more I can take." I can't let him know that I feel a pull toward her because he would egg me on if for no other reason than to win the bet.

"I think that means it's working."

"Oh, it's working, all right. Do you know I passed up two girls at the festival? Two gorgeous women."

Jay chuckles and nods. "That's too bad."

"Then I taught her a song on the guitar." I scrub my face with my hands and groan. "And I liked it. What is wrong with me?"

"It's best not to fight it—just go with the flow."

I point a spatula at him. "Oh, you would like that, wouldn't you? And stop sounding like my mother."

He shrugs as he slings another order slip toward me. "Actually, I would like it for various reasons."

"At least I get a few days off."

After delivering sandwiches to two women dressed in scrubs, I shake my head. "Let's get something straight. Don't start playing matchmaker. She's not my type."

He scoffs. "Oh, look who's jumping to conclusions. I never said that, but since you brought it up, you two are really cute together. And you get this adorable smile on your ridiculous face when she's around."

I scoff. "Don't go there. I like my life the way it is, and I want Beatrice."

"I get that you didn't see a happy home life growing up, but—"

"That has nothing to do with it." I motion toward the growing line of customers. "Stick to taking orders instead of being my matchmaker. Got it?"

His phone rings a Celine Dion tune, and I roll my eyes at the ringtone he set for Hazel.

"Is that the ball and chain?"

"Hush. Hey, hon. What's up?" His smile fades, and he scrubs his hands over his face. "Is she okay? Yes, go. I'll see you tomorrow. Tell Amelia to hang in there."

My ears perk at the sound of her name, and I turn to face him. "What's going on?"

"Nothing."

I hold out my hands to take his phone, but he won't give it to me. "You can't ask, 'Is she okay' then say, 'Tell Amelia to hang in there,' without it being something."

"Man, I can't tell you. She doesn't want you to know, but I promise it isn't about you. The thing she's dealing with is definitely not something you did or didn't do."

That doesn't give me much comfort, and the expression on his face makes my stomach churn. "What happened? Is she okay? Is she hurt?"

He motions with his hand toward the man at the window. "Your customer wants his mustard-free sandwich."

Shoving the sandwich basket through the window to the waiting customer, I turn my attention back to Jay. "Did she hurt her hand again? Is someone in her family sick? Come on, you have to tell me something."

"No, I don't, but I do have to ask you a question."

"What?" I turn the mustard bottle to squirt some on a Beef Cake burger.

After a long pause, he asks, "Will you be my best man?"

I squeeze so hard that all the contents squirt out with such force that they land on my T-shirt and all over my arm. "What did you say?"

He hands me a towel. "We've set the date."

All the blood drains from my head as dread sinks in. "Nooo."

He backs up. "Why?"

Wiping the last of the mustard from the counter, I ponder my next words. "Because it's a trap."

"And I love it." His grin is disgusting.

I let out a whimper.

"Is that a yes?"

"Not unless you tell me what's going on."

He groans then scrubs his face. "Maybe you should ask Axel. But if she finds out I said anything, you will never get to look at Beatrice again."

Something bad happened. I don't know what it is, but I'm going to find out.

With the last customer taken care of and the equipment cleaned and put away, I race home and change clothes. I blasted Axel's phone with message after message until he told me where to find Amelia. He wouldn't say what was wrong, but at least I got that much out of him. I cannot stop thinking about what could be wrong. She could be sick, or maybe it has something to do with Dolly. I just wish she told me instead of leaving in the middle of the night like that. For the first time in a very long time, I want to be there for someone. Amelia's sweet and adorable, and I like her more than I want to admit.

I screech to a halt in Amelia's sister's driveway and bound up the steps to the front door. I bang on the door like I'm trying to break in, and the door swings open. Dorothy, I think, stands there with a little boy on her hip. She looks me over. "What are you doing here?"

I peek over her shoulder in hopes of seeing Amelia, but the little boy bops me in the face with a toy.

"Truck."

I swat it away. "Dorothy, right? Is Amelia here?"

"Truck," the little boy says again, shoving it in my face.

Dorothy adjusts the kid on her hip. "He'll keep doing that until you take it from him."

Holding out my hand to take the toy, I instead get an armful of child as he leans into me and puts his arms around my neck. Before I know it, I'm holding a little boy as he vrooms his truck up my neck and across my head and back.

"Okay."

Dorothy smiles. "He likes you."

I flinch when the truck rolls over my eye. "I could be a kidnapper."

She snorts. "Not hardly." She holds the door open wider. "You might as well come in."

I follow Dorothy through the living room to a bedroom while I carry the boy who acts like he's known me all his life. When I see Amelia lying in a fetal position on the bed with used tissues all over the floor, I freeze. Her puffy eyes and red nose break my heart.

"Vroom, vroom."

I place the kiddo on the floor and softly say, "Amelia?"

She looks up, and when she registers it's me, she abruptly sits up and wipes her face with her hands. "What are you doing here?"

"What happened?"

"Nothing." Her eyes stay trained on the floor.

Dorothy takes her little boy by the hand. "Tucker and I will be in the other room. Amelia, you need to tell him."

"No."

Dorothy lets out an exasperated groan. "He came here because he was concerned. Don't be a jerk."

Amelia gasps as Dorothy and Tucker leave the room.

"I'm not a jerk."

"Of course you aren't." I take a step toward her, but like a scared pup, she scoots away from me. "Please talk to me."

She sniffs and turns her back to me as she whispers, "I can't."

"Please." My hands find her shoulders, making her slump in defeat. "How did you find me?"

"Axel."

She growls as she wriggles my hands off her. "He has a big mouth."

"I had to promise he could play Jay's guitar." Bringing up the ax makes me think of the bet. The right thing to do would be to come clean with her, but it might tip her over the edge today.

"Figures. You know his weakness."

"We all have weaknesses. Even me."

"Pfft. You do not. By now, I would have noticed at least one. But me? I'm... f-f-f-full of..." Her lip quivers.

I close the gap between us and tip her head up with my finger under her chin. "You are my weakness, and I'm not leaving until you tell me what's going on." Swiping a tear from her cheek, I stare into her eyes. "Please."

I have never begged a woman for anything, and usually, when a female is upset, I run the other way. Adding drama into my life is not what I normally do. But normal doesn't exist when Amelia is part of the equation.

She takes several breaths that make me think she's about to hyperventilate, then she bursts into tears as she falls into my arms. She buries her head in my chest. I wrap my arms around her and hold her like our lives depend on my strength.

She grips my shirt as she sobs. "It's... Bennet."

Son of a... "Is he hurt? Dead?"

She takes a deep breath. "He's my ex-fiancé. Claimed he didn't want to get tied down. Wasn't the marrying type." She uses air quotes to emphasize her sarcastic tone. "Apparently, he's getting married. The ceremony is going to be at the Belle Meade Plantation, of all places. That was *our* place."

"Geez." I scrub my face with my hands as I sit beside her on the bed.

Her breath hitches. "Yeah, same place where we arranged our wedding. I have massive credit card debt and a broken heart because of him. Two years later, and I'm still paying off the florist, and don't get me started on the wedding dress." She gasps. "Please don't tell my parents about the dress. I lied and told them I got a refund."

I lean back on the bed and stare at the ceiling, trying to process what she just said. "Let me get this straight. He broke up with you on your wedding day and left you to pay all the bills?"

She nods. "I didn't even want a big wedding. But it wasn't just the wedding, which for most of the stuff, I was able to get the deposits back. It was all the stuff I paid for willingly to try to fit into his world. I kept getting deeper and deeper into debt, and when he called off the wedding, I knew I wouldn't have anyone to help me pay off all the money I spent."

My heart sinks thinking about everything she said. Without overthinking it, I pull her tighter, and she doesn't resist. She melts into my side and closes her eyes.

After a kiss to the top of her head, I say, "I think you dodged a bullet. It's a small price to pay to not be stuck with that douche for the rest of your life." When she doesn't answer, I add, "Especially since it was because of his asshattiness that you met me."

She snorts as she raises her head until we are nose to nose. "So I should thank him?"

My gaze flicks down to her mouth and back to her eyes, and I want to kiss her so badly it hurts. I would probably make things worse, so I force myself not to go for it.

A door opens, and in walks the little boy holding Dolly's leash. He bounds into the room while his mother follows with an infant in her arms. "Sorry, I tried to catch Tucker, but Dolly was about to have a fit to see her mommy."

Dolly paws at Amelia's legs until she gets picked up. She licks Amelia's face as if she hasn't seen Amelia in days.

I clear my throat. "Let me take you back to my apartment so you can relax. I won't even make you sleep on the blow-up contraption."

Amelia chuckles, and I consider that a minor victory. "I think I'll stay here. I need to rethink everything: my business, my living situation, my entire life..."

I glance at Dorothy, who urges me to continue.

"I want to help."

Amelia peers at her sister, who nods her approval.

"Okay. Just give me a second. I have to use the restroom."

While she's in the bathroom, Dorothy approaches me. "She's a mess. I did the best I could, but I'm not sure I made any headway. If I could track down Bennet, I'd give him a piece of my mind."

"You and me both. I cannot believe he dumped her and left her with all that debt."

Dorothy glances toward the bathroom door. "It's worse than that. They dated for two years. I never liked him, by the way. Then they lived together for six months. The day of the wedding, he decided he wasn't marriage material. She lost the condo, the furniture, a fancy car, everything. She was so devastated that she had no fight left, so she just moved out with nothing but a suitcase of clothes and her dog. Dax and I have offered so many times to help her with money, but she won't take it."

My blood boils at how he treated sweet Amelia. I hope to God I never meet him because I won't be able to pretend like I don't know. "He's a dick."

Dorothy snorts. "That's putting it lightly. But instead of being vengeful, Amelia figured out how to turn her sad situation into something good. That's when she decided to make it her mission to transform players like him into people who would want to get married."

I scrub my face with my hands. Instead of being bitter and turning into a man-hater or spiraling down into an ice cream–laden depressed state, she sought to make men ready to take the plunge. My heart swells with admiration and adoration for this woman. I turn to watch her as she meanders through Dorothy's living room like a sleepwalker. Her ponytail is twisted to the side, and her shirt is more wrinkled than usual.

After swallowing hard, I say, "I'll take it from here." I'm not sure what exactly I mean by that, but Dorothy seems to understand.

"You're a good guy." She pats my chest before she leads Amelia to the door.

I'm not sure about that, but I've grown attached to Amelia in the short time we've lived together, and I certainly don't want her to be sad. She's the sweetest, most genuine person I've ever known.

I walk up behind Amelia and put my hands on her shoulders.

She lets out a stuttering sob. "I'm okay. I promise. I won't make you fuss over me. That's not in the contract."

"Oh, hogwash."

I spin her around and pick her up, making her yelp.

"First, we're going home, then you're going to take a very long bubble bath, eat ice cream, watch a sappy rom-com movie, and you can crash in my bed." Our eyes meet, and I let out a deep chuckle. "I'll sleep on the couch, but I won't have you eat chocolate or watch a romance movie all by yourself."

"You'll join me to watch whatever movie I want?"

As I carry her down the driveway with Dolly trotting by my side, I nod. "Anything you want."

"What if I'd rather watch Star Wars?"

My cheeks hurt from grinning so much. "I would say you couldn't get rid of me if you tried."

She buries her head in my shoulder and mumbles, "And the bubble bath? Joining me for that?"

My stomach clenches, thinking about how much fun that would be. But the last thing she needs after being gutted over a guy is for another guy to get cozy with her.

"Don't tempt me, sweetheart."

CHAPTER TWENTY-FIVE
Amelia

We don't speak during the entire ride back to Phin's apartment. I'm humiliated and ashamed that I broke down in front of a client. This has never happened before, but then again, I've never received this kind of news before either.

"You get your comfy bedclothes. I prefer those super-short ones, but..."

That makes me smile, which is not an easy task right now.

He jerks his thumb toward the bathroom. "While you do that, I'll start the bath water. Now, don't be mad, but I might have a few girly bath items tucked away for, you know... The ladies love aromatherapy."

A moan escapes my lips. "I should tsk you right now, but I may never leave the bathroom."

"Scoot."

My eyes well up, and I feel like a failure for crying again. "Thank you." I lunge toward him and wrap my arms around his neck. His arms encircle my waist to draw me close. He feels so good pressed against me, and I wish we could stay like this forever. Right before I lose my nerve, I plant a quick peck on his cheek then rush into the bedroom.

Real professional, Amelia.

It took all my willpower to peel myself away from Phin's protective body. His soft voice and strong arms are exactly what I need. But when he suggested a long, hot bath, I was two seconds away from telling him I was serious about him joining me. Thank goodness the awkward ride home gave me a little time to get my wits about me, but apparently, it didn't do much good since I kissed him on the cheek. *Gah*. I'm hopeless.

I pace in my bedroom, Dolly right at my side as I process my emotions. Even when Bennet left me, I hadn't felt so defeated, but now I know it wasn't just cold feet—it was cold feet with me. That hits me right in the heart. Then Phin had to witness my lowest point, but he came looking for me. He was concerned, and I don't know how to process that.

When I step into the bathroom, I find it converted into a miniretreat that could be a setting for *Southern Living*. Lit candles sit on the edge of the tub, and I smell lavender wafting through the small space. Phin looks up and grins over his shoulder.

"Along with the froufrou stuff, I also found this bathtub caddy." He perches it across the tub then places a glass of wine and a book on it. Almost bashful, he adds, "I don't know if you like thrillers, but this is all I could find."

I clutch my chest, trying to hold my emotions inside. "This is so sweet."

He reaches out. "Give me your phone. I won't have you ruining your recharging session by checking social media or drunk dialing anyone."

"Ugh." I hand it to him. It's like he can read my mind.

He scratches the back of his head. "I'll leave you to soak. If you need anything, just holler. Dolly and I will be stretched out on the couch watching a baseball game."

"She likes the Braves."

"A match made in heaven."

After he leaves and the door clicks shut, I shimmy out of my clothes and sink into the bath with a sigh. My mind immediately goes back to Phin standing in my sister's house, holding Tucker. Even in my emotional state, my hormones surged, and my mind went down a very nonprofessional path. He looked very natural holding that sweet boy. But the pain in Phin's eyes was evident. He was hurting because I was, and that was the sweetest thing a man has ever done for me. When I have a chance, I need to add a journal entry because his ability to empathize is a huge step forward.

I take a sip of the wine and rest my head back on the edge of the tub. When I close my eyes, instead of seeing the dirtbag ex of mine, I see Phin. He may think he's a player, but he's got taking care of his partner down to a science.

Memories of the last few days waft through my brain. The concert, the festival, and even the trip to urgent care were all special because he was there with me. Even after the contract is complete and I move out, I will keep those moments with me always.

After I have soaked so long my fingers and toes are shriveled, I regretfully climb out of the bath, dry off, and slide into my pajamas. Wrapping my robe around me, I step out of the bathroom.

Phin looks up from his phone, and when he sees me, it slides out of his hands and onto the couch. He pats the cushion next to him, and when I sit, he takes my feet in his lap and proceeds to rub them.

My eyes roll back in my head as a moan escapes my mouth. "Oh my, Phin. That feels so good."

"Can this count as extra credit?"

"Absolutely. One more slice of the poodle has been completely removed."

"Yes!" He slides my feet off his lap. "Ready for the movie?"

"Let's do this."

As we settle in for the movie with Dolly between us, I sink lower into the couch.

Out of the blue, Phin says, "I'm sorry about the dirtbag."

"It's okay."

"No, it's not. I don't know how anyone could push you away and treat you like that."

"Thank you." I'm on the verge of tears again, so I focus on the movie. "This is my favorite of all the Star Wars movies."

"Mine too."

Before I can stop myself, I rest my head on his shoulder. He places his cheek on the crown of my head and takes my hand that's petting Dolly. I know I should pull away because he is my client, but I think we have become friends too. I sigh and drink in the moment because I need this so much, way more than I thought.

I wake on the couch to a sleeping Phin scrunched up next to me. He looks ten years younger when he sleeps, with his relaxed facial muscles and partially open mouth. Seeing him like this gives me a glimpse into what he might have looked like as a teenager. I'm sure he was a heartbreaker from an early age.

I sit up and find Dolly asleep in the crook of his knees, where she normally sleeps on me. I lean up onto my elbows, but a large arm surrounds my waist and pulls me toward him.

Phin tucks me in close to him. "Don't go."

"This is inappropriate."

"Nonsense." He snuggles into my hair and purrs. "Don't overthink this. I won't make you sleep on that blow-up contraption tonight. Just sleep." His hand splays over my stomach, and I'm sure he can feel the butterflies fluttering around in it. I know it's just because I'm so vulnerable, but I could stay like this forever.

"If you insist." I let out a deep breath and relax back into him.

He kisses my temple, and I can't hear anything over my heartbeat thumping in my ears.

I roll onto my back and pull his face down until his lips are on mine, and I forget how to breathe. The kiss is slow and soft, and I slide my arms under his T-shirt, enjoying this chance to touch his taut body.

He takes his time, and it's so delicious. If I were standing, I'm sure my foot would pop. I never want this moment to end.

Nothing in my foster-wife manual prepares me for falling for a client, and I don't care right now. Phin makes me feel like the most cherished person on earth, and I need that right now.

He pulls back abruptly. "I'm sorry. I shouldn't. We shouldn't."

"I'm sorry too. I shouldn't have kissed you. I don't know what I was thinking. I'm not even your type." I let out a pained chuckle, embarrassed that I made a move on him when I've done nothing but preach the boundaries of the contract. I have rules for this very reason.

"That's not it, Amie. I know you're not in a good place right now, so this isn't a good idea. Besides..." He blows a raspberry. "The contract."

"You're right." I slide off the couch. "I'm going to my room, and I'm going to read the fine print of our agreement. Good night, Phin, and thank you."

"Good night, Amelia."

I racewalk back to my room and try not to cry. *How did I think any of this would be a good idea?* What an idiot I am. It would have been better if I had never met Phin. Of course, Phin thinks he is falling for me, that I'm his "weakness" like he said at Dorothy's. But that's just the proximity of living with someone. That just means he's ready to fall in love and I am the most present opportunity. They always fall a little in love with me, but I understand the psychology of it, and until now, I've never reciprocated. I'm not his type. If he had real feelings for me, he would have asked to be let out of our agreement. I'm not sure what is worse—being jilted at the altar or falling in love with the sweetest guy on the planet and knowing that he's meant for someone else. Both suck.

CHAPTER TWENTY-SIX

Phin

I flop onto my other side and bury myself in the couch. I should march down to Amelia's room and tell her I want to take her on a date, like a real, honest-to-God date. I want her like crazy. I should tell her I want to end the contract and try this thing for real.

Then I see Jay's face mocking me for being a sap. She does this all the time. This is her job. She makes men fall in love with her so they want to fall in love with somebody else. And she's still hung up on her ex. That's why she kissed me. She was probably thinking of him. My stomach churns, and I hold myself still. I have to keep this in perspective. I am not falling in love with her. This is just what she does. She doesn't care about me. She is only here for the money.

Once I have talked myself off the ledge, I remember that the only reason I am doing this is to win Jay's guitar. With a whimper, I punch my pillow, getting comfortable on the sofa, trying to settle my internal battle with the angel on one shoulder and the devil on the other.

Devil: *She's just a girl. Any girl would make you feel this way.*

Angel: *You know you care about her more than you want to admit.*

Staring up at the ceiling, I need to devise a plan to stay away from her as much as possible for the next few days while I proceed through her steps. I will put a smile on my face, do whatever she needs me to do, finish out the contract, then move on with my life with that awesome guitar by my side. Though, there is no way that guitar will feel as good as Amelia did in my arms. Dammit. I scrub my hands over my face.

Not able to get any sleep, I jolt off the couch and start a pot of coffee. I hope a shower, colder than usual, will help wash away the feeling of her in my arms.

That's not going to happen, because Amelia's bath-time supplies still litter the tub, and I growl at how much I like it. I'm getting domesticated, and it ticks me off. Not waiting for the water to heat up, I dive under the shower's spray. The tepid water cools my hormones, but it doesn't take long before my thoughts slide back to her. I turn the dial all the way until it's nothing but freezing water hitting my head. With lightning speed, I soap and only quickly rinse my hair before I shut off the water. My entire body shivers while I sling on clothes, still partially wet.

Showered and dressed, I fill a tumbler full of coffee and write a note for Amelia. I tiptoe into her room and hope to God I don't wake this angel while I retrieve supplies for the day. She lies on her back on the air mattress with her hair splayed around her and Dolly tucked in beside her. As promised, the poodle poster has lost more of its scruffy pieces, revealing an almost-completely-groomed dog.

I want to rip up the contract right now. I tuck the note under her phone and leave for a long, painful day of work. I feel my man card dissolving in my pocket a little every day.

With my ball cap down as low as possible, I go about my daily work activities. The birds chirping in the tree near the food truck mock me as if to say, *We're happy, and you're not.* Jay's whistling gets on my last nerve. I bet he didn't turn down the most amazing woman on the planet.

"If you don't mind, I have a headache, and your whistling runs through my brain like a song from Captain and Tennille."

"Ha. Good one. I'll try to keep it down over here."

"Thank you." I shove a plate toward Mr. Griffin so hard his sandwich barely stays on it.

He scrunches his brow as he makes his way to a park bench.

"Sorry, man. I just didn't get much sleep last night."

"Ah, I heard all about the meltdown. So, you were the shoulder to cry on, right?"

"Dorothy did that part."

Jay's eyebrows raise. "Oh. What part did you play?"

I chuckle under my breath. "Not what you think."

He hands a customer his receipt and gives me the order slip to prepare the meal. "I just thought from the grumpy-cat face and the fact that your left shoe doesn't match your right might mean the reason is..."

"I didn't get any, either, if that's what you're implying."

He holds his hands out in defense. "I'm not saying anything. But the fact that your mind went there tells me all I need to know."

I glare at him, and he snaps his mouth shut.

After a moment of silence, I ask, "When your cousin worked with Amelia, did he ever indicate he felt like he was getting too close to her?"

Jay shakes his head. "Not that he ever mentioned."

"You know, like... did he ever kiss her?"

Jay slams the cash drawer so hard he catches his index finger in it. After a slew of curse words, he finally calms down enough to answer. "No, he never kissed her. I'm certain of that. Did you?"

I mumble, "Maybe. Technically, she kissed me first, and I was a good boy, so we stopped before it went any further."

Jay whistles. "I don't know what to tell you about that."

"I'm not sure why I even told you. You'll probably use it against me so you can keep Beatrice."

It's like a light bulb goes off in my head, and I turn to face him. "Wait a second. Is this all part of her plan? Was the ex-fiancé getting married and me comforting her a step in her protocol to see if I have what it takes to handle a tough situation?"

"No. Do you really think she could fake that level of sadness? I know Hazel was worried out of her mind over Amelia. This was not a fake breakdown, and you should kick yourself in the balls for thinking it."

I guess not. Amelia seems like a straight shooter, but she could be fooling me big-time. Her sweetness could be an act.

"So, it was just a quick peck on the cheek, right?"

When I don't answer, he lets out another whistle. "Dude. You're falling for her."

"I am not."

"Whatever you say, Mr. Bachelor, but I know love when I see it."

"So you're an expert now, right?"

"I'm not saying that. All I'm saying is I've seen how you've changed this week, and it's all because of one cute dog-fur-covered lass."

I slam the sandwich together and stick it out the window, not caring if it goes to the correct customer. "That is ridiculous. But even if I am changing, and I'm not saying I am, how do you know it's not just me growing up and it has nothing to do with her program or *her*?"

"Man, I've known you a long time. Do you think your transformation is a coincidence? You're changing because of her. And it's not because of her techniques but *her*. Admit it."

All I can do is shrug. His truth bombs make my chest constrict.

"But... you *are* changing for her."

"I. Am. Not."

He does kissy noises, and I want to squirt him with mustard.

"Would that be so bad?" he asks.

"Yes. One word. Beatrice."

"Pfft." He rolls his eyes. "The bet was a stupid idea. Listen to your heart."

"Gah. You sound like my mother."

"She's a very wise woman, so I'll take that as a compliment."

He would. I need to distance myself from Amelia, or I'm going to lose my heart and the bet. I think I would eventually recover from not owning the guitar, but something in the back of my pea brain tells me if I let Amelia in, I may not survive without her.

CHAPTER TWENTY-SEVEN
Amelia

The aroma of hazelnut coffee wakes me up from the best sleep of my life, and it takes a moment before I remember my breakdown then Phin's epic rejection.

I can't believe I bawled my eyes out last night over that bonehead, Bennet. He's not worth tears, but when I found out he was getting married, I lost it. Turns out he was marriage material. He just didn't see me in his future. Now that the sting of reality has faded, I'm glad he didn't want me. It never would have worked permanently between me and Bennet. But still, the harsh reality is a hard pill to swallow.

No sooner do thoughts of Bennet leave me than Phin's beautiful face appears in my mind. And that kiss. It was the best kiss of my life. If he can make someone as simple as me feel completely adored and cherished, imagine what he does to one of those bombshells. I was ready to dismiss him as my client and become a member of the Phin Baxtor Fan Club after just one kiss. It is completely clear now why women fall all over him. And I'm really into him. This is bad. Really bad.

I slap my cheeks to wake me out of my haze. It feels like I've been transported back to tenth grade, when I got partnered with Colin Creed in bio lab. He was so flirty, and I was hooked from day one. It turned out the football linebacker had played me like a fiddle to get me to do all the work. And he was successful, while I didn't dare look at him for two more years.

Phin was so sweet to me with nothing to gain from it, but then he backed off when I kissed him. Stupid me. *Gah!* I wonder, if he weren't my client, whether things would have been different last night. *Who am I kidding?* I am not the type to catch his eye to begin with. He's even commented on the dog hair on my clothes, so I know he's used to more put-together and certainly more voluptuous women.

I sling on some clothes and go in search of coffee. I find a pot brewed but no Phin, thank goodness. I'm still too embarrassed to face him. Maybe tomorrow. Maybe next year.

Dolly enters the room, stretches, then shakes.

Pouring a cup of coffee, I say to Dolly, "What am I going to do about this silly crush?"

Dolly wanders around the apartment then proceeds to go to Phin's room, jumps on his bed, and nestles in. Phin is not going to like that at all.

Without making Dolly move, I get dressed for work and daydream about how it felt to be cared for. Next to my phone is a note from Phin.

Amie,

Hey, lazy girl. I didn't want to wake you because I thought you needed the extra rest after your sucky day. Hope you have a better day today.

Phin.

I clutch the note to my chest. How sweet. Even though he took the easy way out by avoiding an awkward conversation this morning, he left me a note. No guy has ever done that before. I wonder what he does after a second kiss.

As I prepare five kittens for foster homes, Hazel organizes the supplies for each one. She is so good at figuring out which toys each animal prefers.

She starts to hum a tune but stops immediately. "Are you okay?"

"I don't know."

She rubs my arm. "Honey, don't let Bennet the butthead get to you. He's a loser."

I shake my head. "It's not Bennet. It's Phin."

Hazel groans as she places a string toy into the bag. "Oh no. What has he done now?"

"Nothing. He was sweet. He fixed me a bubble bath, complete with candles and wine. We watched a movie together and fell asleep on the couch."

"Did he make a move on you?"

"No. I mean, we kissed, and it was amazing, but I made the move on him." My words are so breathy I don't even recognize my voice.

Her eyes get big. "Oh. Did you two...?"

"No. We both remembered who we are and what our relationship is. But wow." I flop back in my seat, remembering the kiss.

Hazel gets the biggest grin on her face. "That's wonderful. I knew there was more to him than he lets on."

"No, it's not wonderful. He stopped it from going any further. Plus, he's my client. I'm supposed to be getting him ready for his forever home, not sucking face with me."

"It's more than that, and you know it. You're getting him ready... for *you*."

"Nope. It's totally one-sided. He left this morning before I woke. I'm sure he regrets the kiss, and now I've made things awkward."

She looks like she doesn't believe me.

After a deep breath, I say, "I need to set up my next client. If you know anyone else who could use my help, send him my way."

She rubs her temples. "Amelia, maybe it's time to give up this consulting business of yours."

"Why?"

"Because I think it's keeping you from finding your soulmate."

I scoff. "You know I don't believe in that stuff anymore. It got me nowhere but heartache, and my meltdown reminded me of the pain I had been in. I'm not going down that road again. Nope."

Hazel's mouth turns down. "It's a shame because you have so much to offer."

Her friendship warms my heart, and I love having a sister from another mister to help in times like this. "Aw. You're sweet, but I feel like I'm not meant to be married. I'm okay with that. But for now, I need to get over this infatuation I have with my client, who clearly doesn't feel the same as I do, and finish out the contract as quickly as possible. That would be best for everyone involved."

Hazel frowns. "That must have been some kiss."

I plop down in a chair and wipe my face with my hands. "You. Have. No. Idea."

She laughs. "I think you're going about it the wrong way. How do you know Phin isn't attracted to you?"

"I told you. He backed off."

"You want him to change and respect women, and that was exactly what he did."

"Well, when you put it that way..."

"Don't answer for Phin. He's not usually shy about how he feels. Let him tell you if he's not interested."

"Actions speak louder than words."

She snatches the bags and marches away. At the door, she turns around. "You're impossible. But more so, you are a wonderful person, and so is Phin. Maybe something is there, but you'll never know if you stay in your safe little bubble. And this client stuff is just a front to hide your sadness."

Harsh, but maybe it's just a tad true.

CHAPTER TWENTY-EIGHT
Phin

Nothing like driving around in a frickin' food truck for three hours after work so I don't go home to face that gorgeous face. I know it's cowardly of me, but I'm not ready to talk about that kiss with Amelia, mainly because I can't trust myself not to be the one to kiss her this time. On a scale of one to ten, to quote my favorite music movie, that kiss was an eleven.

My stomach rumbles for the third time in less than five minutes, so instead of going home, I pull into a strip mall and make myself a Fowl Sandwich. Sitting in my food truck, eating leftovers from today's menu is ridiculous, but it beats having to deal with the kiss conversation right now.

With nothing left to do and a full stomach, I drive to my mother's house. It's been too long since I've visited the cozy townhome she's owned since I was little. She opens the door, and her grin gets huge when she sees me.

"Phin, this is a surprise. Come in." Flour dusts her hair, making her look like she's got a few gray hairs, and it's a snapshot of what she will look like in about fifteen years.

I enter and am overcome with the smell of chocolate pies baking. I should have skipped the nasty food truck meal and come straight here.

"It's been a while, so I thought I would stop by."

"Come help me with the pies. I'm trying out this new chocolate pecan pie and need a taste tester. Want to be my quality control?"

"Absolutely."

I sit at the bar while she pulls out a set of piping-hot mini pies from the oven. While they cool, she fills more baking tins with pie crust and filling. She slides a perfect pie my way, and I dive in immediately.

"Mom, this is so good." I accentuate it with a chef's kiss.

The kitchen is her happy place. No matter how exhausted she is, she gets reenergized by rolling out dough. My mom taught me that no problem couldn't be solved by slapping some dough on a floured surface and making something edible out of a few simple ingredients.

After a few minutes of silence, she says, "So... how's Amelia?"

I flop my head on the bar and whimper. "Is it that obvious?"

She laughs as she places more baking tins in the oven. "I know you better than anyone, and you've got it bad."

"I do not."

She pops me with her oven mitt. "She's adorable, and you know it."

"And I am her client, remember?"

"Pfft. Ask to get out of the agreement. Tell her it worked. Like, really worked."

I shake my head. "She got some really bad news about an ex, and I was trying to be the comforting friend when..."

Her mouth drops open. "Say no more."

Thank God. Time for a change of subject.

"Have you thought any more about opening your own place instead of helping me and Jay out in our little clunker?" I ask.

"Actually, there's a place on Broadway called Three Point One Four. Ever heard of it?"

Thinking of going there with Amelia and her family causes a warm sensation to run through my body. "Yeah. It's amazing."

"The owner wants to retire, and..."

My eyes get big. "Mom. That's perfect. The location couldn't get any better, and if you continue their menu plus add some of your specialties, you'll be a success for sure."

She walks around the bar to stand next to me and squeezes my shoulder. "I was thinking it might be time you gave up the food truck and worked with me like we've always talked about."

"And sell the truck?"

She shrugs, and her hesitancy sends my heart racing.

"Mom?"

"Yes. I would love if you sold it. Every time I walk inside, I get the heebie-jeebies. Why do you think I help you guys by hanging out with the crowd in the parking lot? Your father... he only did two things right in his life. One was to keep me in his will, even after he left us, and the other was to give me you."

When her voice cracks, I lose my resolve. I hug her. "Mom, I didn't know. Too often I've thought I was—"

"You're nothing like him, except those piercing blue eyes."

I breathe deeply and take in her words. I may or may not be like my father, but after being around Amelia this week, I know I don't want to be like him. And thinking about Amelia reminds me of the bet. Maybe it's time to let Jay just flat-out win.

"I'll think about it."

"Great."

Keeping a secret from my mother is driving me crazy, so I need to come clean about the bet. Mom is going to rake me over the coals, but I have to tell her.

"About Amelia—"

My phone buzzes, announcing an incoming text.

Amelia: *We need to talk.*

At least one of us has the guts to start the conversation.

I kiss my mother goodbye then roll into my apartment parking lot and slog to my apartment. No time like the present. When I open the door, it's quiet. I look around and see no sign of Amelia anywhere. I tip-toe around, and when I get to my bedroom, a furry little head pops up from my bed.

Woof.

I quirk an eyebrow. "Dolly, what are you doing in here?"

She rolls over on her back, tempting me to rub her stomach.

I snap my finger and point at the door. "Go."

She shakes but then burrows into my sheets.

"That is not what I said." I plop down on the bed and fold back the covers. "Out. Now."

Dolly does an army crawl toward me, but instead of jumping down, she puts her paws on my chest then licks my nose. She is worse than Amelia about worming her way into my life.

"You're cute, but I kind of like my women a little taller than you."

Lick, lick.

"Not gonna make a difference."

Lick, lick.

I scoop up Dolly and take her outside to do her business just as Amelia drives up.

When she sees me with Dolly, she freezes. "You don't have to do that. It's not part of the contract. I was going to be out in the hot sun all day, so I left her in the apartment. I hope she didn't—"

"It's fine, and I don't mind. She needed to pee, and I needed her out of my bed."

Amelia giggles. "Sorry about that. When I left this morning, she looked so comfortable I couldn't bear the thought of moving her. I hope she didn't yak on your comforter."

My heart stops beating. "I didn't check. If she did, you'll have to share your blow-up mattress with me tonight." I waggle my eyebrows to bring home my point.

Her face flames with an adorable flush as her mouth opens and closes like she's at a loss for words. She clears her throat. "I wanted you to know that I appreciate everything you did for me last night after I had the meltdown of the century. But I was totally unprofessional... you know... the kiss."

And there it is. She's been thinking about it all day too. Now I'm at a loss for words, especially because that is not what I want to use my lips for anyway.

"Yeah." She stares down at her shoes.

When I open the front door, Dolly leaps out of Amelia's arms to dart right through my bedroom door. Fleabag.

Breaking the uncomfortable, as-thick-as-pea-soup silence, I ask, "So, what's left before I am dashing, perfect husband material?" I rock back on my heels in hopes I sound cockier than I feel, but my attempt to be casual falls flat.

Amelia focuses on the wall behind my head. "We're taking a break, like I said when this debacle started, so we can do something you would like."

"I don't know what that means."

Someone bangs on my front door, and I cock my head.

"Open up you two. My hands are full."

Amelia opens the door, and Layne stumbles in, holding two massive bags from China Dragon. The aroma that fills the room has my stomach grumbling, no matter that I already ate.

I watch as Layne and her belongings take over the apartment. "What are you doing here?"

"I called Amelia to see if she wanted to hang out, and she filled me in on what happened."

My eyebrows raise so much they must be lost in my hairline. "Filled you in about what?" If she knows about the kiss, I will be hounded for the rest of my life. Layne can be relentless when she gets a nibble of information, and it's not pretty.

"About the jerk who will remain nameless."

I assume she's talking about Bennet because if she meant me, I would have felt her wrath by now.

She hands me the bags and squishes my cheeks. "Who knew you had such a soft side?" She smacks me on the cheek. "Amelia's techniques must work."

"Again, what. Are. You. Doing. Here?"

She stares at me like I'm the dumbest person on Earth. "Hanging out. Duh."

The door blasts open again, and in walk Derrick, Gus, and Gus's wife, Danielle. Derrick carries a twelve-pack of beer and plops it on the table.

My friends surround Amelia and pummel her with questions about how she's holding up. I must be in the Twilight Zone because only a few days ago, they hated her.

Amelia's face brightens as she interacts with my friends. "Who's up for poker?"

The room gets deathly quiet. She turns to me. "Too soon?"

"Yeah. How about we just watch the game?"

Derrick lets out a deep sigh of relief. "Thanks. I'm just beginning to warm up to her. Let's not go backward."

Amelia hip bumps Derrick, and now I know I'm in an alternate universe.

CHAPTER TWENTY-NINE
Amelia

Danielle is so sweet, and she is a perfect match for Gus. She sits on his lap as they share Mongolian beef, and it's adorable how he caresses her back while she feeds him like a bird. Layne sits on the floor with her back resting against the couch while she wrestles with a lo mein noodle as it slides off her chopstick. Derrick relaxes back in the recliner and flips channels until he comes to the Braves game.

I drag a chair from the kitchen and sit in it while I devour the best General Tso's chicken I have ever tasted.

Derrick springs out of the chair and high-fives Phin when Dansby Swanson hits a home run. "That's two this game. He's on fire."

"Unlike you in high school." Layne wields her chopstick like a bat. "His timing was so bad, he would strike out looking."

Derrick pulls his cap down low on his face, but it doesn't hide his blush. "It's harder than it looks." When Phin chuckles, Derrick gets a wicked expression. "Remember the time Phin forgot to wear his cup?"

Gus laughs so much Danielle has to hold on to him to keep from falling off his lap.

My brother wasn't the sporty type, so I'm not sure what Derrick is talking about. I glance at Phin, waiting for his reply. He stuffs his face full of food and chomps down.

"Cup? Like a..." Derrick's meaning dawns on me. "Oh... I bet that was not pretty."

Gus whistles. "I'll say. His balls blew up like softballs."

Layne doubles over laughing, and Danielle swats her husband on the shoulder.

Through her laughter, she says, "That was not nice."

Derrick fwaps the recliner to a sitting position and takes his empty food container to the trash can. "See, Amelia? I'm not being a slob this time."

"I noticed."

"I still don't like you very much."

I stand and hug him around the waist. "Yes, you do. Admit it."

He wraps his arms around me and squeezes. "Maybe just a little."

Phin clears his throat and cocks his head. "Do you mind taking your hands off my foster wife?"

"Oooooh," Layne says. "Getting protective, are we?"

He clenches his jaw. "He's a flirt, and she doesn't need that right now."

"Aw," Danielle says. "Phin, that's the most sensitive thing I've ever heard you say."

Phin points to the television. "Let's just watch the game."

When our eyes meet, Phin motions for me to sit next to him on the couch. I settle in between him and Gus, and every time Phin jumps up to celebrate a good play, he returns to the couch a little closer to me.

He whispers in my ear, "You doing all right?"

"Yep. This is good."

"Good."

He slides his arm around me, and a warm, gushy feeling flows through my veins. His hand combs my hair and plays with a strand, making me wish we were alone but at the same time glad we aren't. He's still in the comforting mode, and I don't want a repeat of last night's mistake kiss. Two days in a row of rejection from him would be more embarrassment than I could handle. I can't let my feelings get the best of me, so I rise from the couch and go to the kitchen in search of anything to cool my hormones. Phin being all touchy-feely and sharing his friends is getting the best of me.

I open the refrigerator for no other reason than to have the cool air shock my system back into reality.

From behind me, a soft voice says, "Anything wrong?"

I swing around to find Phin standing right behind me. Shaking my head, I do my best not to look him in the eye. "A little thirsty."

His smiley eyes turn smoldering, and my heart won't stop beating out of my chest. "Are you sure? My friends can be a little..."

"Amazing."

He stares into my eyes, and the wheels in his brain churn. "You like them?"

"I love them. I was wrong about them." I swallow hard and stare at the floor. "Your friends are part of your family. Not kennel cough."

Phin lets out a husky laugh.

"You'd be lost without them, and they care so much about you. Gus is a good role model, and Derrick is not the player he thinks he is. Neither are you."

He laces his fingers with mine, and when I get the nerve, I glance back up at him.

"I'm not a player," he says. "At least, I'm not anymore. I... you have—"

Derrick and Layne scream at the television, bursting the bubble Phin and I were in. He clears his throat and releases my hands. "I better make sure they didn't break anything."

"Yeah."

While he saunters back into the living room, I stay fixed in my position. Derrick and Gus describe how Dansby Swanson caught the ball with his bare hand and threw for a double play while I try to wrap my brain around what just happened in the kitchen. I don't care about baseball right now, and I can't wait until the game is over and his friends leave, because a lot remains unsaid between Phin and me. I'm feeling things I shouldn't for my client, and if I'm not wrong, he feels them too. He may have pushed me away last night, but tonight, he is doing anything but that.

Layne appears to get the hint. "I think it's time to go."

Derrick's face falls. "There are two innings left."

She plants her hands on her hips. "They're ahead by ten runs. Time. To. Go."

His shoulders slump, but he extracts himself from the recliner and fist-bumps Gus and Phin.

Danielle stands. "Us too."

Gus's jaw drops. "Seriously? But..."

She raises an eyebrow, and he snaps his mouth shut. "See ya, bro."

Danielle and Layne give me hugs and last words of encouragement as they leave, making a lump form in my throat. Other than Hazel, I haven't had much in the form of friends, especially after Bennet left me. Not only did he take everything I owned and left me with debt, but my friend group was his, and bros before hoes, so it's been lonely without a good group.

Phin closes the door behind the last of his friends and scratches the back of his head. "That was awkward."

"Thank you for letting me borrow your friends. I want you to know I did not invite them. Layne is kind of like a freight train when she gets her mind set on something."

"Ha. You have no idea. But it's okay. I think they like you."

"I like them too."

He takes a step toward me, and I know he must hear my heart pounding out of my chest. Phin stares at the ground and mumbles something. After a deep groan, he says, "Want to finish watching the game?"

That was not what I was hoping would come out of his mouth, but I'll take what I can get. "Sure." While I settle down in the recliner, I type a quick journal entry on my phone.

Journal Entry 5

Phin continues to progress, but since the last few days have been off schedule due to unforeseen circumstances, he's pivoted nicely. And so have I, for that matter. Phin's friends have warmed up to me, and I feel like one of the group, which is bad for business! But on a personal note, I enjoyed tonight more than I should have let myself. I know I'm getting my hopes up, but I like Phin. Phin, the client, has almost completed the program, and I need to put an Elizabethan collar around my heart to protect myself from the pain I am about to feel.

After the game, I suggest a movie because I don't want this night to end. Instead of a romantic moment, it ends with Phin asleep on the couch next to me, his heavy head resting on my shoulder. I slide the sleeping Phin to my lap and play with his hair as soft snores come from his partially open mouth. My phone buzzes, and I lean over to retrieve it, doing my best not to disturb Phin.

Layne: *How are you doing?*

Me: *Much better. Thank you for coming over.*

Layne: *I practically had to drag Derrick out of there. He cannot read context clues.*

Me: *It's all good.*

Layne: *I hope I'm not disturbing you.*

I snap a picture of Phin drooling and send it to her.

Layne: *LOL. In all the years I've known Phin, I have never seen him asleep in someone's lap. You have him smitten.*

Me: *He's so cute when he's asleep.*

Layne: *He's in love.*

I bite the inside of my mouth to keep from squealing. It can't be possible that he feels the same as me. Phin has awakened something inside of me I didn't think was alive anymore. This wasn't in the plan, to fall for my client, but this feels so much different and way deeper than anything in my past. For the first time in my life, I feel cherished and possibly loved.

As soft snores come from his mouth, I play with his hair while Dolly snuggles at his feet. Since he is completely zonked out, I switch to one of my favorite movies to pass the time. While Sandra Bullock does her best to tell the family she is not engaged to their comatose son, I stare down at Phin. He's way better looking than Peter Callaghan and certainly kinder than Jack. When it gets to the part about Peter having only one testicle, I giggle, even though I know the line is coming.

Phin stirs in my lap. "What are you watching?"

"Only the best movie in the whole wide world. *While You Were Sleeping.*"

"Never seen it."

I gasp. "That's wrong on so many levels."

He leans up on his elbows and stares at me with sleepy eyes. He is so adorable with this dreamy expression. "What time is it?"

"Midnight."

"Have you slept at all?"

"Too wired to sleep."

He rolls onto his back so he's staring up at me. "You didn't take any incriminating pictures of me, did you?"

I cringe. "Maybe."

He sits up on the couch and scoots me down until I'm lying flat. He rolls me on my side and settles in behind me. "You'll have to sleep like this so I can be sure you don't do anything else without me knowing." Sliding his hand around my waist, he breathes into my ear, "Let's get some sleep."

Like I can sleep now. I can hardly breathe!

Every muscle in my body tenses as my brain stops working.

"Relax. I'm not going to cop a feel."

My shoulders shake with rumbles of laughter. "And just when I thought you were turning into a gentleman…"

"Oh, I am many things. You've been warned."

With a hefty dose of confidence, I say, "Is that a promise or a dare?"

He leans up, and before I know what's happening, he's on top of me. "Amelia, I want to kiss you so bad, but…" His nose grazes mine.

"But what?"

"But I don't want you to be mad at me."

In a wispy voice, I reply, "I promise."

"Good."

His lips crash into mine, and I snake my hands around his waist, pulling him closer. His groan sends tingles down my spine all the way to my curled toes. As he trails little kisses down my neck, I tighten my grip on his waist then slide my hands up to remove his T-shirt. He flings it across the room, and I run my hands up his bare chest.

He purrs in my ear. "What song on the REO Speedwagon album *Wheels Are Turnin'* is about a man's fear of change but knowing he needs to?"

I rest my head back on the cushion with the biggest grin on my face. "Is it 'Can't Fight This Feeling'?"

With more kisses on my neck, he mumbles, "Mm-hm."

"Only you would use someone else's words, but I'll take what I can get."

His laughter rumbles in my ear as he teases my senses. He leans up and stares into space.

"What's wrong?"

With our foreheads pressed together, he mumbles something unintelligible. "I need to tell you the truth about something."

Here we go. He's treating me like all the other girls. I fell under his spell, and now it's time for the letdown. He's had his fun and is ready to send me packing. Except, we haven't even had any "fun" yet. I fight back tears because I don't want to let him know what I'm feeling. I need space, so I push him off me and stand.

Phin hooks his fingers into the belt loops of my jeans to pull me closer. "I have never known anyone like you."

Staring at my feet, I swallow. "That's probably a good thing."

"That makes you even more special." He stares off, and I sense his emotional conflict. After a deep breath, he says, "Tomorrow, let's figure out what to do. I have some things I need to clear up because I don't want to ruin this."

I cock my head to the side, not quite sure what he means. "Are you hiding a girl—"

"No, not at all. I like you, Amelia. So much. I just don't want to screw up."

"Fair enough."

With his arms around my waist, I feel like nothing can go wrong.

CHAPTER THIRTY

Phin

Dolly licks my face and makes me come to my senses. My back is stiff from my awkward position on the couch. I have been wedged between the back of the couch and Amelia for the bulk of the night, not that I mind, but it would have been way more enjoyable in a bed. I extricate myself from the couch and already miss the warmth radiating from Amelia's body. She rolls over and lets out a sexy, sleepy sigh, but otherwise, she's out like a light. Dolly takes off toward my bedroom, and I'm sure I'll find her in my bed, buried deep in the covers. Somehow, that doesn't bother me—much.

As quietly as possible, I tiptoe to retrieve my T-shirt then head into the kitchen to pour myself a glass of water. I pull out my phone from my pocket and check the clock. It's nowhere near time to start the day, as is evident by the big yawn that escapes my mouth, but I am wide awake. My brain and heart fight one another, and I am pretty sure my heart is going to win this battle, which doesn't scare the crap out of me at all.

As soon as I get to work, I need to call off the bet with Jay. Even if he considers it a win for him, it's a win in my column too. Anything I need to do to have Amelia is well worth it. Never have I wanted someone so much, even more than a stupid guitar. My mother will be proud of me, right after she rips me a new one for the bet I made.

"Hey." Amelia leans against the kitchen doorframe. With her messy hair and sleepy smile, she looks good enough to eat.

I place my phone on the counter and close the gap between us like an animal on the prowl, and I guess I am. "Did I wake you?"

"Sort of, but I'm awake now." Her flushed cheeks are adorable.

Picking her up, I plant her butt on the counter and snuggle between her legs. "You should probably go back to bed."

She slips her hands around my neck and takes a deep breath. "To sleep?"

My forehead rests against hers, and I breathe in sync with her. "I didn't say that."

Amelia purrs, and if I weren't turned on already, this would do it.

"Amelia."

"Yes, Phin?"

"The box of business cards in the closet?"

"Go on."

I take a moment to collect my thoughts because I don't want to blow this. Nothing is more of a buzzkill than talking about your exes in front of someone you care about. "Each one of those cards was a woman who only wanted fun for a short time. They never cared about getting to know me. And yeah, I didn't care about them, either, because none of them were worth a second glance. I'm not sure why I feel like I have to explain myself, but I do."

She bows her head and takes a deep breath. "Go on."

"I guess I didn't think someone out there could really get me until I met you. I never thought I could ever want more than one date with a woman, but you... I want lots of dates. Lots more time with you. Lots of doing nothing together."

A tear trickles down her cheek as her breath hitches. "That is the sweetest thing anyone has ever said to me, but are you sure? I'm a hot mess."

I cradle her adorable face in my hands and run a thumb over her lips. "No take backs. I'm serious. Where have you been all my life?"

Amelia cocks her head. "I've been trying to get men to see their full potential."

"Yeah, what are we going to do about that?"

"What do you mean?"

"I might get a little jealous if you go off to live with another guy when I want you here."

"Oh." She looks off into the distance. "Are you sure you're not just worried about Dolly? I mean, I've noticed how smitten you are with her now."

I throw my head back and let out a huge laugh. "Maybe. Probably not. I'm serious. I hate to admit this, but I think your techniques work. They probably worked a little too much on me for your liking."

She strokes the back of my neck then shakes her head. "Not at all. I never thought—well, after Bennet, he..."

I kiss the words out of her mouth and hopefully out of her mind. The last thing I want her to be thinking about is that jerk.

She wraps her legs around my waist and squeezes them, pulling me in closer. I suddenly feel alive again. I untuck her T-shirt and slide it over her head then sling it over my back. Scooping her off the counter, I carry her down the hallway and into my room.

Woof.

Amelia giggles as I plant her feet on the ground at the foot of the bed. A tail sticks out of the sheets and wags like crazy. Dolly crawls out and stares at me with the cutest puppy-dog eyes.

I point at Dolly then jerk my thumb over my shoulder. "Out."

Dolly burrows deeper into the covers.

In a deep, growling voice, I say, "Dolly..."

She peeks her head out with her ears pulled back then looks at Amelia.

"Sorry, little buddy. Three's a crowd. Go."

With that, Dolly stands, shakes, and hops down to trot out of the room as if she knows what we're about to do.

"Where were we?" Amelia asks. She walks up to me, and with a feathery touch, she picks up the hem of my T-shirt and glides it over my head. Each time her fingertips graze my skin, it sets off every nerve in my body.

I slide my hands down her arms, making her shiver. With a flick, I unlatch her bra, and it slips down to hang from her wrists.

In the living room, Dolly yips.

With her mouth on mine, Amelia mumbles, "Ignore her."

"Gladly."

I remove her bra from her hands and fling it behind me while she wrestles with the waistband of my basketball shorts. She seems as hungry for this as I am, and as cheesy as it sounds, I really can't fight this anymore.

With Amelia wrapped around me, I don't ever want to move, but Dolly paws at the bed. If I thought growling at a dog could work, I would, but she's more stubborn than her owner. I lower my arm over the side of the bed, and when I find her fuzzy face, I give it a gentle nudge to move her.

Dolly whines, insisting I get up from my warm, cozy cocoon. After one more peck to Amelia's cheek, I slide out of bed and cover her. Amelia turns over, taking the comforter with her. While I tug on my underwear and basketball shorts, Dolly runs to the front door. As I fling on my T-shirt wrong side out, I hear someone pounding on the door.

Through the peephole, I see Mom standing there with her phone to her ear.

Worst timing ever.

I open the door, and Mom lets out a huge sigh. "Oh, thank goodness. You weren't answering your phone."

She lunges toward me and wraps me in a big hug. "You always answer. And you're never late for work."

"I was... busy." And I won't go into any further details with my mother.

"Do you know what time it is? Jay has been worried sick. You didn't answer your phone, and he couldn't leave or he would lose the truck's spot for the day, so he called me."

I pick up my phone, which must have slid off the counter during our prelude to sex, and check the time. "Oh, crap. I'm late, and I have the truck." My phone has blown up with text messages from Jay.

"Yeah. What were you doing?" She cocks her head as she waits for my answer.

"Stuff," I say as I scan my messages from Jay and Mom.

"Stuff? As in girl stuff?"

I cringe because it looks really bad.

She shakes her head. "Oh, Phin. What is Amelia going to think?"

We stand there staring at each other. I hold my hands out, hoping she connects the dots.

When the gears click into place, her jaw drops just before she does the sprinkler dance, which no one should ever do, especially her. "Forget about work."

"Forget about that dance."

She pops me on the arm. "This is amazing."

My face feels like it's on fire, and I don't think I could grin any bigger. "I think so."

Mom takes me by both shoulders and gives me a shake. "Don't mess this up."

It's time to come clean with Mom. She's going to be so disappointed in me, but I can't keep this from her any longer. "Yeah... about that. Mom, I gotta tell you something. I haven't been completely honest with you, and I need your help making things right."

I take her by the hand and lead her to the couch. There's no easy way to say it so I squeeze my eyes shut and blurt, "I made a bet with Jay that if I hired Amelia and didn't change, I would win—"

"Win what?" Amelia's question from behind me sends a shiver down my spine. I turn at a snail's pace to see her standing in the living room, wearing my Rolling Stones T-shirt. Her face is ghostly white, and her hands are clenched at her sides, making her knuckles blanch.

When I don't answer, she asks, "Phin?"

I glance at Mom, who motions for me to continue. "Son, what have you done?"

Too terrified to face Amelia, I stare at my mother. "If I completed the program and did not change, I would win his vintage guitar."

In slow motion, Mom covers her face with her hands. "You have got to be kidding."

"I wish I were." I scrub my face and stand to address Amelia. This won't end well. "You know how much I love music."

From behind me, Mom says, "I'm going to leave this to you and Amelia, but I am so disappointed in you." Her words gut me because I would rather have my fingers cut off than let my mother down.

After the door clicks shut, I focus on Amelia again. She cocks her head to the side as she crosses her arms over her chest, waiting for me to continue.

I swallow hard. "Jay has this smoking-hot guitar that I would kill to own. Anyway, after you worked with Jay's cousin, Jay wouldn't stop yammering on about how much it worked, so I decided to prove him wrong."

Her eyebrows pull together. "About what?"

"That your techniques don't work. So I bet him I wouldn't become marriage material even after I let you work your magic on me."

Her eyes grow distant like she's processing my words. "I see. What happens if you changed?"

"He gets the business."

"Wow. You must have been pretty confident." I can almost see the wheels turning in her brain and clicking into place. She walks up to me and pokes me in the chest. "This was all a bet? You had no desire to be a better person."

"Wait, that was before—"

"Oh. That pity make-out session the other day and then last night... it was all just your usual gotta-get-laid mentality." Her breaths come short and shallow, and I'm afraid she's going to pass out.

I reach out to touch her arm, but she snatches it away.

"That's not true. I had plans to tell him the bet was off today because—"

"I cannot believe you. I thought you were something special." Her voice cracks, and it breaks my heart. "I broke my number one rule."

"What was that?"

She stares at the ceiling and lets out a deep sigh. "I fell for a client." Amelia quietly walks across the hallway to her bedroom and pulls her things out of the closet, with me following right behind her.

"What are you doing?"

She throws on a sweatshirt and some shorts then stuffs a bag full of the rest of her clothes. "I'm leaving. Our work here is done. You owe me nothing. In fact, I will refund you the deposit." She drops her belongings and with a quivering breath, she says, "I'll get this stuff later. Let me know when you won't be here."

I touch her arm, and she jerks away like contact with me stings. "Don't touch me."

"Amelia, I *have* changed. I lost. Don't you see?"

A wicked chuckle comes from Amelia, something I haven't ever heard from her before. "Save that for your next bet."

"That's not fair."

Her spine stiffens. "I was completely honest with you from the start, and you played me like your precious vintage guitar. I'm not sorry you lost the bet. I hope you lose the guitar *and* your food truck. Have fun finding a job and a girl who doesn't want a commitment. The only thing I got from you was heartache and a sliced-up hand."

"Please don't leave."

"Goodbye, Phin."

With a tear-stained face, she shoves past me, and Dolly follows her out of the apartment and out of my life. The sick feeling in my gut is far worse than food poisoning, and no amount of puking will relieve me of the mess I've made. I should have called off the bet earlier. It was a dick move to make the bet in the first place. I'm a mangy, untrainable dog that deserves to sleep alone for the rest of his life.

With a dead feeling in the pit of my stomach, I drive at a snail's pace to the park, reliving last night's amazing sexy time then having it all come crashing down around me this morning. My life is screwed up. Amelia gave me a chance to be a better person, and I ruined it. I threw it all out the window like scraps from a leftover sandwich.

When I pull up to our usual spot in the park, I find Jay sitting on the hood of his car, holding our slot so some other food truck doesn't horn in on our usual place.

He throws his hands in the air and yells, "Where the hell have you been?"

I park beside him and slide out of the driver's seat, hanging my head lower than a dachshund's belly.

Jay scrunches his brow when he gets a good look at my forlorn expression. "You okay?"

I scrub my face with my hands. "I had a rough morning. She's gone."

"Amelia? Why?"

"The contract is over."

"But you two... I thought you hit it off with her."

I let out a huff. "Doesn't matter."

"You told her about the bet, didn't you?"

"More like she overheard me coming clean with Mom. And it was after we..."

His mouth forms a big O, and we stand there in silence for a moment.

"You might have wanted to do those steps in reverse order."

I wave him off as I pull out the condiments and ready my workstation for the customers already lining up. "Can we just focus on the customers?"

He mumbles something as he slides a ticket down the wire toward me.

"It never would have worked anyway."

He points the iPad stylus at me. "You are not your father."

"Pfft."

"I'm serious. You are a decent person, and when you care for someone, you do it with your whole heart. And the reality is if you didn't, you wouldn't be so worked up over Amelia leaving. The Phin you want people to see would be planning a night out at the club to find your next plaything." He shivers. "What has Hazel done to me?"

I chuckle, but deep down, I appreciate what he's saying. "Thanks, buddy."

"Truth hurts. You are a great person. You're smart, funny, and one of the nicest people I know. Plus, you own your own business."

Slamming the mayo bottle back in the holder, I hold out the sandwich for the customer. "A business I don't have anymore. A bet is a bet. We'll deal with that another day. Just focus on work today."

I may be doomed to be a permanent bachelor, but at least I have my friends, and I can always count on them to be there for me.

CHAPTER THIRTY-ONE
Amelia

It's hard to keep my car between the lines from all the tears blurring my vision. Dolly whimpers from her carrier in the passenger seat.

"I'm sorry, Dolly." My breath hitches as I wipe my face dry. "He fooled me too."

My phone buzzes nonstop, but I don't want to talk to him, ever. I barely eked out three words before I gave up trying to explain to Dorothy on the phone while driving toward her house. I am so stupid. Phin played me like a fiddle, and I didn't even see it coming. I fell for all his charisma, looks, and lies. I told myself I would never let that happen again, but I guess I never learn.

And I can still feel his hands touching me, his warm breath on my neck, the way we seemed to be in sync with each other's wants. *Ugh.*

When I pull into Dorothy's driveway, Ramona's and Laura's cars are already there. *Gah!* It takes all the energy I can muster to walk into the house. As soon as I open the door, my three sisters surround me in a group hug, and I cry my eyes out, again.

Ramona wipes the tears off my face, and with a down-turned mouth, she says, "I'm so sorry. Let's have a sleepover tonight, eat lots of ice cream, and bash men."

"All men except for me, I'm guessing."

We all turn to see Axel in the doorway holding a twelve-pack of Southern Grist, my favorite local beer.

"Who called you, and isn't it a bit early to start drinking?" I ask as I fall into his open arms.

"It's the typical Day family hotline. Dot called Ramona. Ramona called Laura, and Laura called me. I'm pretty sure Hazel and Liberty are on their way too. And on days like this, it is *never* too early to get inebriated."

Axel squeezes me in a big bear hug then leads me to the couch. I sit between Laura and Dorothy with Ramona on the love seat. With my family around me, I sniffle as I wipe snot from my nose with my sleeve. I don't even care if it's gross. They've seen me do far worse.

"I thought he was different." My breath catches as I try to say more.

Ramona hands me a tissue box. Leave it to the nurse in the family to think of germs and hygiene. "You've had clients before that you knew wouldn't change. What's different about this one?"

While I stare at the floor, the room goes silent, then one by one, they all say, "Oh."

Axel sits in front of me on the coffee table, taking my hands in his. "You love him, don't you?" He breaks the silence with his cut-to-the-chase question.

"Nope." I add, "I think I was just infatuated. He's handsome and full of charisma. That's what it was. I'm sure of it."

He lets out a deep sigh. "Sis, I saw you with him. He couldn't take his eyes off you. After the concert, he wasn't able to keep his hands off you either."

"He loves women."

Axel shakes his head. "But—"

I hold a hand up to stop Axel.

He groans and rubs his face. "Sis, he... fit."

"He's a flirt. He does that to anything with two X chromosomes. Besides... he made a bet against me."

Laura's head jerks around, and her mouth falls open. "Come again?"

"The whole thing was a wager with Jay. The entire time, he was doing what he had to do just to get through the steps. If he made it through the contract and didn't change his behavior, he was supposed to win some stupid guitar."

"What guitar was it?" Axel asks, and his four sisters stare at him like he's lost his mind. He slinks back into the couch. "Okay, too soon, and I think I figured it out. It was *that* one."

Dolly jumps into my lap and licks my face. She hates it when I'm sad.

"I do love him. I mean, I did. He's worse than Bennet."

Dorothy scoffs. "No one is worse than Bennet. He's a dog." She cringes. "Sorry for the reference. I know that's part of your system."

Wiping my eyes and blowing my nose, I sit up straight. "You know what I need to do?"

"Call him and let him explain?" Axel gets a serious stare down from four angry females.

"No. I'll line up my next client. Right after I refund that scummy fleabag's money. It's tainted. I can't keep it." I pull out my phone and send the refund to Phin, but he immediately returns it. "Uuugh. He's so annoying. He won't take the money."

Ramona snatches the phone from me. "You are not going to use this thing today. Dumped dialing is worse than drunk dialing."

"I was not dumped. I was lied to."

"Doesn't matter. I am going to hide this so you don't get tempted to send anything to him."

I huff and cross my arms. "Fine."

For the longest day in eternity, my siblings stay by my side. I have to beg them to let me use the restroom by myself, but even though I do need to use the bathroom, I also need a moment to myself. The person staring back at me with her puffy red eyes and messy hair looks exactly like how I feel. I never thought I could feel lower than when Bennet left me or when I found out he was engaged again, but I was wrong. This is ten times worse, and it's all my fault.

I plop back down on the couch as Dorothy's thumbs fly across her phone, then she claps her hands. "Okay, pizza is on the way. Thanks to Axel, we have beer. What movie?"

"Star Wars," we all say at the same time. No matter which one we watch, we'll spend the next ten hours quoting it and debating which set of movies is best.

While Dorothy gets the plates, Dax walks in with the sweetest niece and nephew known to man. Tucker runs to me and wraps his tiny arms around my neck, making me forget my troubles for a short moment.

Dax takes Tucker from me. "Sorry about what happened."

"Thanks."

"I'll take the kids into the playroom so you Days can do your therapy session." He kisses his wife then takes the kids to a back room.

Ramona loads *Star Wars: A New Hope*, and I already feel better. She knows it's my favorite.

Axel nudges me with his knee. "I'm sorry it didn't work out."

"Me too. I thought he had promise."

He rolls his eyes. "I'm not talking about with Phin, the client. I'm talking about it not working with Phin, the guy who had a great time at the concert with *you*, the one who comforted *you* when you found out about the evil one, and the same one who looked at *you* with hopeful puppy-dog eyes all the time. I'm telling you, sis. He cares for you."

"He likes to play the field. I don't think he would ever settle down and certainly not with someone like me."

Axel leans forward and stares at me. "What's that supposed to mean?"

I wad up the tissue and pull out another one. "I am not like the women he fawns over. They are tall and leggy and have perfect hair." I touch my rat's nest to confirm I will never fit the bill. "And they certainly don't have dog hair all over their clothes, so whatever silly girl crush I had on him is over. Done."

"It's more than a crush, and you know it. If it was just a crush, you would be angry but not messed up."

"I'm not messed up." I hate the way my voice rises while I try to lie to myself and my sweet brother.

His eyebrows raise, and he lets out a slow whistle then whispers, "Did you and Phin...?"

"Shh."

"You did, didn't you?"

My sisters whip their heads around to home in on my conversation with Axel.

Knowing I can't keep anything from them, I blurt, "Fine. We did it."

Laura high-fives Dorothy. "Pay up."

I gasp. "Y'all bet on me too?"

They stare at one another, then Dorothy says, "Maybe..."

"Ugh. You're all awful." But deep down, I know they love me and always have my back. "Let's watch the movie. I want to focus on decent men for a while, and I think Luke and Han will fit the bill."

Axel shrugs. "I don't know about that. Han was pretty rough around the edges at first."

"I'm not waiting around until Phin gets out of carbonite to find out if he has feelings. Not happening."

I'm so mad at Phin right now I could scream. Dolly licks my face, and I give her a squeeze. Even though she fell for Phin, I won't hold it against her. He's good at what he does.

Journal Entry 6

The contract between myself and Phin Baxtor is completely dissolved due to his inability to fulfill the agreement. Phin is the first client to sign with me who hasn't been open-minded about the process and was, therefore, unable or unwilling to change his behaviors. His refusal to take the commitment seriously has resulted in me returning his funds immediately, terminating the professional relationship.

I'm not sure if Phin can commit, and I fear his resistance to commitment is much more deeply rooted than that of anyone I have worked with. Given the fact that he is unwilling to change, I have to close his case permanently. He may not ever be ready to commit to a long-lasting relationship, and that would be a shame. The person he keeps buried is a great man, but unfortunately, no one will likely see that side of him.

If the client is happier being a forever bachelor, I should be happy for him too. He got what he cherished most out of the contract.

CHAPTER THIRTY-TWO
Phin

If possible, I feel worse than I did yesterday. She won't answer my calls or return my texts. I know where she's staying, but if I go to Dorothy's, I might make things worse. She hates me, and I don't blame her. So all I can do is focus on one sandwich at a time. Hopefully, no one will be too picky today.

Jay clears his throat. "Look who graced us with his presence today."

I glance up to see Mr. Highfalutin standing in line. He checks his watch then scowls at his phone. As usual, his suit looks like it just came from the cleaners, and his shoes don't have a single scuff mark. In typical fashion, he bumps his way to the front of the line because "he's going to be late for a very important meeting." I hope I never come across as that self-centered.

In a flat voice, Jay asks, "What can I get you?"

The man scours the menu as if he's going to choose something different this time. "I'll take a Fowl Play sandwich, extra crispy, no ketchup, and put two layers of paper underneath."

Jay mouths the order as Mr. Highfalutin says it, and it gives me a fleeting memory of Amelia and how badly I messed everything up.

When the dude walks away, Jay says, "Cheer up. At least you aren't him."

I almost smile. "Have a good day," I mumble to the customer in front of me then ask Jay, "What gracious tip did he bestow on us this time?"

"He was feeling generous. A whopping seventeen cents."

"I hope it didn't break the bank."

Staring at the stingy guy, who takes an entire park bench to himself, Jay says, "I don't envy the woman who winds up with him."

"He probably wouldn't break her heart." I sense someone at my window, so without looking up, I say, "The order line is—"

I swallow my words when I realize it's Axel scowling at me, first in line. A long trail of customers I don't recognize line up behind him.

"Why did you do it?" he asks.

"I'm sorry. It was a dick move. I know that now."

"It sure was." He sighs. "Amelia is the sweetest person on the planet. Everyone loves her. Well... everyone with a brain."

"I deserve that. I know it doesn't change anything, but I was going to back out of the bet when I realized how I felt about her."

He holds his hands out as he shrugs. "Too late for that."

"So... are you still interested in a jam session?"

Axel chuckles and shakes his head as he walks backward carrying a violin case. "No. Are you that tone-deaf?"

He stops at the first person in line and whispers something to him then shakes his hand before doing the same to each person in line. The man next in line steps up to the truck with a massive scowl on his face.

Jay asks, "What can I get for you today?"

"My name is Carter. I was Amelia's first client."

Uh-oh. I glance at Axel, and he nods as he crosses his arms over his chest.

Carter stares at the whiteboard showing the menu. "I'd like to order a Fowl Play sandwich, a Pardon my French fries, and a Coke."

Jay rings up his order. "That will be seven fifty, please."

He snaps his fingers. "I almost forgot. What album was the first to be pressed into a CD?"

I look at Jay, who replies, "*Thriller*?"

The guy grins. "Nope. It was *Born in the USA* by Bruce Springsteen." Rocking back and forth on his heels, he says, "I guess that means I get my meal for free."

Everyone in line claps.

After I do a quick Google search to verify the correct answer, I reply through gritted teeth, "Good job and congrats."

Jay slings the order slip toward me, and I begin to fill the order.

Next in line is a fireman. Before I can ask him for his order, he says, "I'll have the Beef Cake burger. Make it two. And my trivia is to name the first to release an album exclusively on the internet."

"U2?" I reply before Jay gets a chance.

"Ha! Nope. It was Prince. I'd like to add fries to that."

The line erupts in cheers as I notice Axel leaning against a tree, grinning like a proud papa. This is his doing. I can sense it in my bones.

A man in a slick business suit is next in line. "I'd like to have one of everything on the menu. What is the most downloaded song recorded in the twentieth century?"

Jay and I glance at each other. "'Beat It.'"

The guy shakes his head, and the entire rest of the line yells, "'Don't Stop Believin'!"

I bang my hand on the counter as everyone in line cheers.

Axel saunters up and pats the man on the back. "What can I say? I know music, and you messed with the wrong musician's sister."

I think I'm going to hurl.

Axel walks away but freezes in front of Mr. Highfalutin. The dude looks up at Axel then stands abruptly. He holds his hands up in surrender, but that doesn't stop Axel from punctuating every word he says to the guy with a massive poke to the chest. The guy flinches, but Axel then waves him off and walks away in a huff.

When the lunch crowd dies down, Jay pops me on the back. "How much did we make today? Ten dollars?" In a girly voice, he adds, "That was super fun."

"Gah." I snatch the ball cap off my head, wipe my brow with my forearm, and tumble out of the truck. "I need to get some air."

I wander around the park and try to clear my head. In the distance, I hear a single violin playing "Hey Jude," and it beckons me to come closer. As luck would have it, the violinist is Axel, who sways with every note. When he finishes the tune, several people clap and leave money in his open violin case. I feel the need to add to the stash, so I toss in a five-dollar bill.

"Man, I'm really sorry. I never wanted to hurt her."

"And yet, you did."

I scrub my face with my hands. "I've got to make it right."

Axel chews the inside of his cheek. "I don't think you can. She's completely broken. You shouldn't have made that bet."

After a deep breath, I reply, "I know. Again, I'm sorry."

He places his violin back in the case and picks it up to leave. As he walks away, he says over his shoulder, "It's not me you need to apologize to."

Long after he's gone, his words still haunt me. I broke Amelia. I hurt the sweetest, most endearing person on the planet. Axel is right. I am tone-deaf.

CHAPTER THIRTY-THREE
Amelia

It was a stupid idea to come to the animal shelter today, but I've cried too many tears over Phin already. I can't let him ruin my heart and my passion, so I drag myself in and hope no one asks questions.

As the day wears on, my sadness turns into anger. By lunchtime, I could spit nails, and Hazel is wise to stay out of my way. For the most part, I stay focused on all the critters that need to be processed for adoption or foster care, with Dolly at my feet. Completely oblivious to the barking all around me, I tap out an email to a new client on my laptop. I bang so hard on the keyboard that I scare poor Dolly. She jumps up, shakes, and settles back down on the other side of the room, and I don't blame her one bit. Phin has made me a mixture of angry and heartbroken, and the latter makes the first even worse. I should have known better than to fall for his tricks. Every single thing he said, every caress, every kiss was carefully planned just to zip through the steps so he could win that stupid guitar. I've got to hand it to Phin. He's the best player I have ever met.

Hazel knocks on the doorframe of the conference room. "I come in peace."

"Of course you do. You didn't do anything wrong."

She slumps down into the chair in front of my desk and scratches Dolly's head. "I had no idea about the bet. I would never keep that from you."

"I know. It's just that in the back of my mind, I knew something was up, but I couldn't put my finger on it. He would do things to purposely make me want to back out of the contract, and I guess when that didn't work, he went full speed ahead to make me think he had changed."

"Jay thinks Phin *did* change."

I stack adoption forms on my desk and staple them with all my force. "Pfft. I don't know what Phin's deal is, but he doesn't deserve to find his soulmate."

She leans forward and rests her elbows on my desk. "You don't believe that. No matter how difficult your clients get, you always feel they have potential."

I wag a finger in her face. "That's because they all sought me out and were ready to be different."

Hazel leans back in her chair and crosses her arms over her chest. "Then one might say it wasn't your techniques that changed those men but rather right timing."

My jaw drops open. Hazel has always been supportive of my system, so her words both surprise and offend me. "You know I helped those guys."

"And they paid handsomely for the privilege."

I stand up so fast my chair slams into the wall behind me. "I can't believe you said that. If it weren't for me, some of them would still be living a meaningless life."

She rolls her eyes, which causes mine to well with tears. It's one thing to lose a client but totally different and painful to hear these words from my most trusted friend.

Hazel sighs and stares at the ceiling. "Amelia, I love you like a sister, but men are ready for marriage when *they* are ready. If Jay's cousin wasn't already in that mindset, he never would have sought your consultation." She holds her hands out in defense. "Sure, you smoothed out some rough edges, but he is the man he always was, just more grown up. That's all."

Her words sting but have some truth behind them. I swallow hard. "So Bennet..."

She looks down at her hands. "He just wasn't ready when he was with you. It wasn't you. Timing is everything. Any man would be the luckiest in the world to be at your side."

My shoulders slump as I drop back into my chair, no fight left in me. I let out a deep sigh as tears fall down my cheeks. "What's wrong with me?"

She rushes around my desk and takes my hands in hers. "Nothing is wrong with you. You have the kindest heart, and anyone else would have turned the Bennet fiasco into a man-hating mission, but you see the good in people and all their potential. I'm sorry if I hurt your feelings. I know your heart is in the right place. And I'm so sorry about Phin."

Barely above a whisper, I say, "Me too. I broke my first rule." I stare at her and shrug. "I fell for a client."

Hazel grabs me in a hug, and I sob onto her shoulder. Dolly jumps up and whines. She always knows my feelings. I don't know how I let myself get into this predicament, but here I am, feeling lower than I did when Bennet left me.

She pushes me away. "Okay. You get this last day to feel lousy, then you are going to get back on your feet and look for the next client. You have bills to pay no matter how you feel."

I shake my head. "I think I'm done. You're right. It was a stupid business anyway. I'll tighten my belt and maybe get a job with Dorothy's husband like he offered. It's boring and mind-numbing, but it's stable. I'll save every penny I can so I can pay off my debt. The foster-wife consulting business is officially defunct."

"If that's what you want, then I think it's a good plan. And if it helps, no more food truck Tuesdays."

I swipe away a stray tear. "That's for sure. I don't think I'll ever eat from a food truck again." I full-body shiver. "I shared a room with a restaurant-sized refrigerator. Do you know what it's like to sleep with that loud humming in your ear all night?"

Hazel giggles. "I would not have lasted one night."

"And the blow-up mattress. Ugh. He was trying to push every one of my buttons right from the start, and he did a great job at it."

"You have to hand it to him. He put a lot of effort into trying to get rid of you, but the funny thing is, when the going got real, he stuck it out. And that look he gives you every time he's in the same space as you…" She lets out a breathy sigh. "That's real."

"Don't care. Lesson learned. I'm done with men, and I'm done trying to fix them."

Maybe it's time I tried to fix myself instead.

My phone pings with an incoming message.

Phin: *Tomorrow night would be a good time to get your things. I'll be out.*

Me: *Gladly. If I have time since I'm so busy with other clients.*

If he can lie, so can I.

Phin: *I am sorry.*

No, he isn't.

Journal Entry 7 - Final

The foster-wife consulting business is no longer in effect. From now on, men are on their own if they want to become marriage material. If they are so motivated, they can research tips. That's what the internet is for in the first place.

CHAPTER THIRTY-FOUR

Phin

Since she's gone anyway, I invite Derrick, Gus, and Layne over for a game of cards. That's what I do because I'm a single man who can do whatever he wants. I instinctively lower the toilet seat and scold myself because I feel like I've been housebroken after all. Not that it makes a difference anymore.

When my friends show up, Layne cocks her head. "What's up with you?"

I furrow my brow and lower my head. The last thing I need is for her to start reading my mind. "Nothing. Let's play."

While I shuffle then sling cards across the table, Derrick chuckles. "Man, what's got your dander up?"

"Nothing."

"Where's Amelia?" Gus asks as he scans his cards.

Layne leans to peek at Gus's cards, and he holds them closer to his chest.

"I thought for sure she was 'the one' after seeing how in tune you were to her needs. You've never done that in all the years I've known you," Layne says.

"And she seems sweet." Derrick rearranges his cards.

I stare at the ceiling and groan. "Guys, she's gone. I messed up, okay? Can we just play cards?"

The three of them glance at each other, then Derrick places his hand down on the table. "Dude, as much as I love having one final straggler like me who isn't married, she seems different, and you know it."

Slamming my cards on the table, I huff. "She is—was—different, but it doesn't matter. She hates me, and I deserve it."

Derrick's eyebrows raise. "Fine. Then, I guess you won't mind if I ask her out."

My heart pounds in my chest, and heat flames my ears. Through gritted teeth, I reply, "Go for it."

His eyes twinkle. "I think I will."

We lock eyes, and I say, "Please don't."

Popping me on the shoulder, he laughs. "I wouldn't do that to you. Besides, I think you need to figure out how to make things right."

"I tried."

Layne groans. "Knowing you, you probably just said 'I'm sorry,' and when she didn't accept your apology, you gave up."

Staring down at my cards, I mumble, "Something like that."

Gus rolls his eyes. "You have so much to learn."

Layne pops me on the arm. "You're stupid. Make a grand gesture. If you care about her, and I mean really care about her, then do everything in your power to win her back."

"Geez, you sound like my mother."

She sits tall in her chair and grins. "I'll take that as a compliment. Your mother is a class act."

"I thought I told you not to talk to her anymore." I play my card and wait for Gus to reveal his.

"I've always talked to her about everything. If I had a mom like Viv, life may have been different, easier."

I scrunch my eyebrows. "You're so much like a super-annoying cousin."

Layne flicks me on the nose, and I swat her hand away. "Exactly. I'm the cousin you need in your life to tell you when you're making the biggest mistake of all time." She punches me in the shoulder for added emphasis, making me wince.

While she and Derrick play their hands, I mull over her words. "I'll think about it."

She puts her remaining cards on the table. "I'm out." She turns to me. "Okay, what's the plan?"

"I have an idea," Derrick says. "How about a sappy card?"

We stare at him and wonder how he could come up with such a lame suggestion.

"Okay, a card *and* a rose?"

Layne stares at him. "Stop talking."

Gus says, "How about a couple's massage?"

"With my luck, she would share it with someone else, so no good." The thought of her with anyone else sends a shiver down my spine. I have to try something, but I have no idea where to begin.

The silence in my apartment is deafening. Amelia only lived here briefly, but in that short time, I got used to her chatter and even her scrappy dog. Dolly wormed her way into my life as much as Amelia did, and the emptiness inside me is enormous.

I pick up the box of business cards and toss them in the trash. They haven't done any good for me, and even without Amelia in my life, I can't keep using those past bad experiences to taint any future relationships. Maybe Amelia would be proud of me.

The pit in my stomach spreads. I can still smell her shampoo, and the candles in the bathroom taunt me. Scooping them all up, I place them in a box and set it next to her stuff in the spare bedroom. When she shows up and sees I'm still here, she's going to kick my butt into next week anyway, so I might as well punch it into overdrive. I never had plans for tonight anyway because I want to explain everything to her, and I hope that if I catch her off guard, she'll have no choice but to hear me out, so I lie down on the blow-up mattress and wait. Maybe these last few days have given her some time to think things through.

The door clicks open, and her soft footsteps pad down the hallway. When she opens the door to her bedroom and sees me lying on her mattress, she backpedals out of the room.

"No way, you jerk. You said you wouldn't be here."

I flop my legs in the air in an attempt to get off the mattress while I yell after her. "Amelia, don't go!" When I catch up to her, I touch her arm.

She snatches it away with the force of a giant. "I need my stuff, so get your lying ass out of that room to let me retrieve it. Then, you'll never have to see me again."

I block her exit with my hands on each side of the hallway. "Is that what you want?"

"Yep." She pops the *p* for emphasis, but she won't look me in the eye.

The dread sinks into the pit of my stomach, and it surprises me how much her words cut me to the core. "It's not what I want."

She scoffs as she scoots under my arm. "That's too bad. Just go back to your life of playing the field and making bets."

I follow her into the living room as she retrieves one of Dolly's squeaky toys. "It was stupid of me, I'll admit. But I don't want to play the field anymore."

She points Dolly's toy at me. "I don't care. You'll be a yard dog for the rest of your life."

"Will you stop with the dog analogies? It's emasculating, especially the neutered part." I feel my balls shrink with every word that flops out of my mouth. "I'm not covered in fleas. I do not have an infection, and my friends do not have kennel cough. Yeah, I finally read the contract."

"It's a little late. Don't ya think?" She storms past me to the bedroom and stuffs her clothes in a suitcase and zips it shut then points to the box of candles. "I am not taking that."

"Please take it."

"Why? So every time I wind down with a luxurious bath, I think of *you*? No way, buster."

I could only dream she would think of me.

She stomps toward the door. "If I left anything, just throw it away." With a loud bang, she slams the door behind her and walks out of my life.

CHAPTER THIRTY-FIVE
Amelia

Curled up on my sister's couch, I do my best to watch television, but all I really do is flip through the channels. One hundred eighteen channels of pure junk. Dolly lets out a woof, signaling she needs to go outside. I rise from the couch and catch a whiff of three-day stink arising from my armpits. After the altercation with Phin, I haven't moved off this couch except to take Dolly out when she's whined enough for me to budge. My hair is a rat's nest, and I don't care if Dorothy gets a letter from the homeowners' association about unsightly visitors.

I open the door, and Dolly bolts out like she hasn't peed in days, but instead of doing her business in my sister's yard, she runs across the street and takes a big dump in the association president's yard.

"No!" I yell as I rush across the street to stop her, as if I could stop her midpoop.

"You pick that up!" Mrs. Kingsman says as she marches outside with her phone, snapping photos along the way.

"I'm so sorry. Let me get a poop baggie."

Dolly takes the opportunity to kick her back legs behind her in an attempt to cover up her excrement.

"Stooop!" I yell at her.

Mrs. Kingsman gasps. "The landscaper was just here yesterday, and the lawn was in perfect shape, but now this." Her nose scrunches as she points to the little dog pile no bigger than my little finger.

Dorothy, with her youngest on her hip, runs out into the street. "What is going...? Oh. Bev, we'll clean this up. You'll never know anything happened."

"Your sister knows we have an ordinance against dogs running loose. You're supposed to keep your critter on a leash when out of your yard."

That is the last straw. I pick up Dolly and try to push the tears down. I've had enough. I don't want to do this anymore. I am a complete and total failure.

Mrs. Kingsman scrutinizes the lawn where Dolly kicked up a divot. "Oh my God. You've ruined my lawn. I'm sending you a bill. You may not care what you look like, but this is my property, and I care."

"Fine, fine. Send me a bill. I said I was sorry." I run across the street and deposit Dolly in the house, collecting paper towels and a doggie bag. The tears fall faster than I can swipe them away. "I am such a fraud. I can't even manage to properly take care of one little dog," I mutter as I rush back across the street. I fall in front of Dolly's tiny poop and scoop it into the bag. I then work on the grass, wiping the residue of her poop from the immaculate lawn, unaware that the words I started as I crossed the street are still tumbling from my mouth. When the divot is replaced, I fall silent, without the strength to rise.

"Oh dear." The woman's shadow moves toward me. "I'm..." At a loss for words clearly.

Dorothy puts her hand under my elbow. "It's okay, Mrs. Kingsman. She's just had a really bad couple of days."

The last words that tumbled out of my mouth were "The guy I love only wanted me for a b-b-bet," and now they run on a loop inside my head. I gather the poop bag and the paper towels and let Dorothy pull me to my feet.

"That's right, Mrs. Kingsman. I've had a really bad couple of days." I wipe my snotty face with my sleeve and take a deep breath. "So if a dog turd on your lawn is the worst thing that happens to you, consider yourself blessed. I don't even have a lawn. I have nothing." My anger flares, mingling with embarrassment.

"We've worked hard to have this lawn."

I raise my hand to stop her. "I work hard too." I turn, walk back across the street, and dump the refuse in the trash can.

I do work hard. But my business is a flop. My love life is a wreck, and the only thing I want to do is volunteer at the shelter. I was so stupid to think I could help other people. I can't even help myself.

With Dorothy's arm around my shoulders, we retreat into her house, and she scours my hands with soap to remove any fecal material that might be there.

"Thanks."

"Did you mean it?"

"I meant every word. I am tired of people like Bev—"

She lays a towel beside the sink. "Not that. Did you mean you are in love with Phin?"

Scrubbing the hide off my hands, I mumble, "I don't know what you're talking about."

"Pfft. You love him, and you know it. Yes, he was a jerk to make a bet, but once he got to know the real you, he couldn't help but love you back. He'd have to be an idiot to not see everything good about you."

"Bennet didn't."

"And he's a jerk. See? My theory is accurate."

My phone buzzes, and I groan. "If that's Phin again, please reply that he needs to take a jog through a rottweiler's yard carrying a juicy steak."

Dorothy checks my phone on the counter and shakes her head. "It's from the jerk."

"Which one? You might have to be more specific. They keep piling up."

She turns the screen toward me. "It's Bennet. He wants to meet you to talk."

I snatch the phone out of her hand and stare at it because she must be pranking me. After reading his text message, I curse myself for not blocking him or changing my number, and I'm doubly mad that my stomach is all knots and butterflies just from seeing his words.

Before I can talk myself out of it, I reply to his message. *Why?*

Bennet: *Unresolved issues.*

Me: *Where do you want to meet?*

Bennet: *30 minutes. In the park at your favorite spot.*

As if he even cared about my favorite spot before now, and I thought it was *our* spot. Typical. Nibbling on my fingernail, I send back a thumbs-up emoji and dash down the hall to shower the three-day funk off my body.

Right when I close the door, Dorothy says, "Don't do it."

He thinks he can come crawling to me, but that ship has sailed. I can't wait to see him grovel and beg for me to take him back. No matter how sad I am, I'm not that sad to go back and live that mistake again.

While I wait for Bennet to arrive at the fountain in the park, I check to make sure I am the most appealing I possibly can be. My skirt is short, my blouse is tight, and my toenails, poking out from my sandals, are painted a bright pink. He's a sucker for pink nail polish. I cannot wait to crush him in front of everyone and let him know I am totally over him.

The aroma of burgers catches in my nose, and I look up to find the source. When my eyes land on Phin's PB&J food truck, I want to scream. Of all the times to meet and in all the places, it has to be here where I'm sandwiched between two jerks—like a jerk Oreo, but without the sweet filling.

Bennett greets me with a hesitant smile. Even though he wears his corporate attire, he sits next to me at the fountain, which is a shocker because he never lets one speck of dirt near anything Armani. "Hi."

I glance at him, and darn it, he smells as good as he looks. "Hello."

He clears his throat. "I know nothing I say will make things right, but I wanted to explain myself and apologize for hurting you."

With a fake smile planted on my face, I say, "No worries. It was for the best anyway. We wanted different things."

"Yeah."

"How long did you feel that way?"

He watches several children race past us on scooters, having the time of their lives. "A long time, and I should have told you that. I just wasn't feeling it. But nothing is wrong with you."

I snort. "That's up for debate, but I appreciate you saying it. So, you're not here to beg for a second chance?"

Bennet shakes his head and chuckles. "No."

I pretend to wipe sweat from my brow. "Whew. I really didn't want to throw you in the fountain, because you only get one chance at all this." I wave my hand in front of my body as if it's a grand prize.

He laughs harder and pulls an item from his coat pocket. "I did want to give this back to you."

In his hand is the four-carat engagement ring I threw at him when he broke up with me. "I want you to sell it or give it away, whatever. I know I left you in a mess emotionally and financially, and I'm so sorry. This should catch a hefty price, so you can start over debt-free."

Something is not adding up. He wouldn't just give me a call out of the blue because his conscience was eating at him.

I cock my head to the side. "That's very generous of you, and it would go a long way to get me out of the debt, but be honest with me for once. Why are you here now?"

He blushes and fidgets, which makes me force back a satisfied grin.

"Well, Rebecca has this friend, and somehow, word got back to Becs that I kept the ring I gave you. She was furious and was ready to call off our wedding if I didn't do the right thing."

My mouth drops open at his confession. Although I knew the idea had to be more deeply rooted than one just of an altruistic nature, I inwardly roll my eyes that this Rebecca girl has so much control over his life and she can make him ask "how high" when she says to jump.

"That's very kind of you. When you get a chance, please thank Rebecca's friend."

His eyes grow big as he takes a step backward. "Oh no. I'm keeping my distance from Layne. She's like a human tornado."

That she is if it's the Layne I know!

Just as he's about to drop the ring into my hand, one of the kids bumps into him. He drops it onto the walkway in front of us, and it pings into the grass. He may be a sophisticated corporate man, but he was never very coordinated. I throw my head back with laughter at how some things never change, and I am so relieved he doesn't want a second chance.

CHAPTER THIRTY-SIX
Phin

"I've been thinking about the bet," I say to Jay as I notice Amelia walking toward the fountain. Maybe she's coming to talk to me. If so, I will grovel, beg, roll over, whatever it takes to make it right.

"Man, don't worry about the bet."

"I want you to have the truck."

Jay shakes his head as he takes the next customer's money. "I'm not taking the truck, and that's that."

I scratch the back of my head. "Okay, how much do you have in your pocket?"

He digs into his jeans and pulls out a wad of one-dollar bills then places them on the counter. "Looks like a whopping seven bucks."

I snatch up the money. "Sold for seven dollars."

"But—"

"No buts. I've decided to go into business with my mother. The truck is yours one hundred percent if you want it."

His jaw drops. "Is this a prank?"

I let out a chuckle. "Nope. It's yours for seven bucks."

Jay's Adam's apple bobs as he swallows while he processes my words. "I don't know what to say."

"Just say you'll buy the desserts Mom and I make at our bakery."

He lunges toward me and grabs me in a bear hug. "Thanks, bro, and I'll let you play Beatrice any time."

"Sweet!"

Layne walks up to the truck, grinning like she just won the prize pig.

"What are you doing here? Don't you work on the other side of town?"

She glances around then shrugs. "I had more important things to tend to."

"'Sup, Layne. What can I get you?" Jay asks.

"A Fowl Play sandwich and a thank-you."

Jay darts his eyes toward me. "I don't follow."

Layne winks at me. "You will soon enough."

While she waits by the truck for her food, Amelia's gentle giggle flitters through the air, and we both turn to see her at the fountain, talking to Mr. Highfalutin of all people.

"What's he doing talking to *my*—I mean—her?"

Layne gasps. "Oh, you didn't know?" She bats her eyes, pretending innocence. "That's Bennet."

All of a sudden, the pieces fall into place. Mr. Highfalutin is Bennet, the one who broke Amelia's heart, or he's at least one of the men since I meet that description also. He's the guy who broke her heart, the same tightwad bastard that's been stiffing us on tips for a year. The way she throws her head back to laugh threatens to send the contents of my stomach up my throat. Amelia can't possibly be talking to him. I let out a string of curse words.

"What is wrong with you?" Jay asks, and he hands a credit card back to our customer.

I point toward the fountain. "Her. She's over there with *him*."

Layne watches with amusement in her eyes. "So, what's it to you?" she asks. "You obviously aren't interested in her." Sarcasm drips from every word.

"Why does she have to rub it in my face, right here in the park?"

"Because it's a public place. Just stick to the orders." Jay motions toward the order slips piling up in front of me.

I glance up again, and when I see Bennet get down on one knee, I slam the knife onto the counter. "Oh no, you don't."

With one large leap, I bolt out the window of the food truck, getting stuck halfway. I wiggle until I free myself, losing one shoe in the pickle bin. Layne pins herself against the truck to avoid my impulsive behavior.

"Dude, we have a door!" Jay yells while I stop, drop, and roll on the ground.

"And he sticks the landing," Mr. Griffin says while others clap.

"Woo-hoo!" Layne yells. "Don't screw up this time."

"Gotta go." I take off as fast as one shoe can take me toward Amelia. "Stop!"

Amelia and Mr. Highfalutin-slash-Bennet, who is in the middle of standing, snap their heads my way just as I slip on some wet grass in my sock and stumble like a drunk but right myself just as I reach them. With one large smack, I hit his hand, sending the large diamond ring sailing into the air to land in the fountain with a splat.

"Don't do it, Amelia."

Bennett fishes around in the pond in search of the ring, and I hope he ruins his suit in the process.

"Phin, what are you doing?"

I bend at the waist to catch my breath and hold up a finger for her to give me a second. Once I can breathe and talk at the same time, I stand up straight. "Don't marry this guy. You can't."

She crosses her arms over her chest. "Why not?"

"Because I love you."

There. I've said it. I finally said the three most terrifying words in the English language when they are connected into one sentence, but it's the truth. I take her trembling hands in mine. "I have loved you since the day you moved into my apartment."

"Wait," Bennett says. "You've been living with the food truck guy?"

Amelia puts her finger to her mouth to hush him then turns back to me. "If so, why did you—"

"I'm sorry about that. I should have called off the bet, but I kept hoping you wouldn't mean the world to me. You did, and you do, and I can't live another moment without you."

She scans my body, from my grass-stained shirt to my muddy knees and all the way to my feet. "Where's your shoe?"

I point over my shoulder at the truck. "I sort of lost it when I jumped headfirst out the window."

Her mouth drops. "You do have a door on that thing."

I chuckle. "Yeah, but it's more romantic this way, don't you think?"

She nibbles her bottom lip. "I don't know what to think."

"You can't marry him. He can't love you the way I do. I love everything about you. I love your crazy, involved family, your smile, the way you laugh... I love every damn thing about you. I love the dog hair on your shirt. I even love your *dog*. Can you believe that?"

Her mouth twitches just a tiny bit.

"I love how you have such a big heart and want everyone to reach their full potential. You could have turned into a man-hater when this idiot left you, but you didn't."

Bennet says, "Hey, now."

Amelia gives him the death stare, and he must know better than to say anything else.

She swallows then says to me, "Go on."

"I don't have a big, fancy ring, but I'll sell everything I have if that's what you want. Of course, I don't have much anymore since I just sold my food truck to Jay for seven dollars."

Her eyes grow big. "You did what?"

Bennett whistles. "I would have given you twenty."

Amelia rolls her eyes and asks me with a shaky voice, "Are you done?"

A tear trickles down her face, and I swipe it away.

"Please, give me another chance. Please, don't marry him."

She glances at Bennet, and they both bust out laughing. She giggles so much she has to sit down on the side of the fountain. Bennett bends over, holding his stomach as he belts out a laugh.

"What's so funny?"

Bennet stands up straight and squeezes my shoulder. "Man, I wasn't proposing. We were just clearing the air."

"You were kneeling with a ring in your hand. That's not clearing the air."

My focus ping-pongs between the two, and neither seems as upset as I am.

He dusts off his knees. "Dude, I am not trying to win her back."

Amelia scoffs. "I should be offended, but I'm somehow okay with that declaration."

Bennet stares at me. "I was giving her the engagement ring so she could sell it."

My head snaps toward Amelia. "Is that true?"

With her hands covering her mouth, she nods. "I'm sorry. I should have stopped you earlier, but you were on a roll, and quite truthfully, you deserved it."

He hands her the ring, then she takes a step away from me.

She's leaving? "Where are you going?" My voice cracks like a pubescent teen's.

Amelia throws her shoulders back. "I need to think." She stuffs the ring in her purse and walks away.

We watch her until she is on the far side of the park.

I turn to Bennet. "What just happened?"

He shakes his head then pops me on the back. "One piece of advice. Fight for her. She's worth it."

"I almost broke my neck getting over here. I was literally hanging halfway out of my food truck. If that's not a profession of love, I don't know what is."

He chuckles. "I wish I had seen that. Dude, you're a mess. Get cleaned up, and if you love her, I mean really love her, don't stop trying." He taps me on my temple. "You have to think like her. She's a dog person."

Bennet salutes me and walks away as he straightens his suit jacket. For the first time in days, my mind is completely clear on what to do. Leave it to Mr. Highfalutin to help me come up with the most Amelia-specific idea that has the best chance of working.

"Hey, I have a piece of advice for you too!" I yell at his retreating frame.

He stops and waits for me to finish.

"Tip better, you frickin' tightwad."

Bennet gives me a thumbs-up and leaves me with his words ringing in my ear like an LP record getting stuck. *Think like her.* Climbing out of my food truck window was easier than that. It's time I develop a plan to win her back.

CHAPTER THIRTY-SEVEN
Amelia

Hazel holds her side as I tell her about what Phin did yesterday in the park. He was so darn cute, and I couldn't sleep all night thinking about his expression of love and how I stood there blinking like an idiot. His actions could have been out of jealousy or the real thing, but whatever it was, I was not about to throw myself into his arms, even if that's what I wanted to do. He blew up my phone with text messages last night, but I ignored them all because I needed time to think.

"So, you didn't say it back to him?" Hazel asks.

I bow my head. "No, I was too shocked."

"Jay says he's a mess."

"Join the club."

Joni, the receptionist, walks into the work room. "Amelia, your brother is here."

Scrunching my brow, I ask, "What's he doing here?"

She shrugs. "He said something about adopting a dog. I mean, that *is* what we do here."

I walk out of the room to the reception area to find my entire family. In all the time I've volunteered here, my family has never stopped by, ever. "What are you all doing here?"

Mom hugs me. "I want to adopt a dog."

"Me too," Dorothy says.

"Your homeowners' association president is going to flip out if you get a dog. You'll be on her naughty list every day."

"I want one too." Axel wraps an arm around my shoulder.

I roll my eyes. "You can hardly afford to feed yourself, much less an animal. It's a huge, lifelong commitment."

"I know, but we were thinking we could adopt the same dog."

"Oh, that's a really sweet idea." I motion with my head toward the door that leads to the kennels.

Axel motions to Hazel, and she nods then scoots ahead of us. "We have some great dogs, and you know I'd love to take all of them home. What kind would you like?"

"I'd like one that has dark hair." Dorothy has a wide, suspicious grin on her face. "Lots of dark, curly hair."

"Blue eyes," Laura says.

My family is so strange. "That's not easy to find," I say.

She shrugs. "Well, I want a very special dog."

"I could probably keep an eye out for that special dog. Sometimes it takes weeks or even months to find the right one."

"No!"

I jump back from them all protesting at once. "Okay, let's see what we have."

When we get to the first kennel, I say, "This is Bailey. He's been fostered a few times, but no one has connected with him yet. He's kind of skittish but super sweet."

The little pug hovers in the back of his kennel. I turn to my family, and they shake their heads.

"Okay. This is Skittles. He's a purebred poodle, so he won't last long, so if you like him, I suggest you snag him today."

"Nope."

A bark comes from the far end of the kennel room, and it's loud and unusual for a dog bark.

"Oh, let's go see what that dog looks like." Mom tugs me toward the back.

"But what about Skittles?"

Axel nudges me forward, and I turn to snarl at him. "What is up with you?"

He takes me by the shoulders and turns me around to face the last kennel on the right. My heart beats out of my chest when I see Phin standing in the kennel, holding a sign that says, Adopt Me.

"Woof."

I slam on the brakes, and my lungs stop working.

Axel whispers in my ear, "Hear him out, please."

I jerk up my chin and walk toward the door that separates me from Phin. "You look right at home in there. Would you kindly tell me what you're doing?"

He sings the lyrics to "Puppy Love," and I bite the inside of my lip to keep from crying.

When I can find my voice again, I say, "I never took you for a Donny Osmond fan."

"It's a Paul Anka song. I'm shocked you didn't know that."

Axel murmurs, "That's true."

I shove my brother away as Phin takes a tentative step toward me.

"Amelia, you rescued me once. All I ask is that you do it again, but this time permanently. I need you. Will you... adopt me?"

Phin takes a tiny jewelry box from his pocket. Laura and Dorothy do the girly "Aww!" as Hazel takes my arm and leads me to the door and opens it. She gives me a tiny nod, and I step inside.

After a deep breath and with the little resistance I have left, I say, "I need to ask you a few questions first. I don't adopt just any yard dog."

His mouth twitches. "Fair enough."

"Do you have fleas?"

His grin grows, and boy, have I missed that smile.

"Not anymore. I'd gladly wear a flea collar on my left hand for the rest of my life if you think it would help."

I snort a laugh. "Are you house-trained?"

He looks up at the ceiling and mulls over my words. "Mostly, but I am trying. I'm getting better at leaving the toilet seat down, so that must count for something."

Axel whispers to Laura, "The dude is already neutered."

By the "Oof" that follows, I assume she gave him a good nudge in the ribs.

I bite my lip to keep from smiling. "One last question. Will you require a lot of attention and playtime?"

He belts out a laugh, and with one motion, he wraps his arm around my waist and pulls me toward him. "I will require a lot because I don't do well if left alone for a long time, especially at night. Are you up for it?"

Tears well in my eyes, and his laughter falls silent.

"I didn't mean to make you sad. Amelia, I'll do anything—"

I shake my head. "It's not that. I never thought I'd be a failure."

"You are not a failure."

I sigh. "I mean, I'm a foster failure. It's when a person falls in love with their foster animal. And I am one hundred percent a failure."

He takes me in his arms and kisses me, making me light-headed.

"I'm so glad you failed."

"Me too."

Phin swings me around while my family cheers. He puts me down and opens the jewelry box. It's a simple single-stone ring, and I love it.

"I know this isn't much, but I didn't have time to order what I wanted to get you. The final set will have four smaller stones surrounding an upside-down heart to make the shape of a..."

We lock eyes, and I know I have found my soulmate. "A paw print?"

With a bashful grin, he nods as I leap into his arms.

Phin didn't need to change at all. He just needed the confidence to trust somebody with his heart. I was the one who had to change. I had to stop putting life on hold by trying to save other people. In a flash, I see how the company was my way of putting a wall around myself. Never again. I will never close myself off from the man I love. We'll make a pawfect forever home for both of us.

Acknowledgments

To my awesome editors, Angie Gallion Lovell and Amanda Kruse. You two believed in my story as much as I did. Thank you so much for helping me get this scruffy manuscript ready for adoption.

To my awesome critique partners: Jamie Smith, Kelly Hopkins, and Jessica Calla. I can always count on you three to give me great suggestions as well as unwavering support.

To Erica Lucke Dean, my RAP mentor. Sorry (not sorry) for all the questions. You are amazing.

To Lynn McNamee for believing in my novels. I am so thankful I found Red Adept!

To Mark, Maddie, and Jethro—I have the best family in the world. Thanks for finding your own dinners! I love you so much.

To the Nashville Humane Association for the inspiration for this story.

About the Author

After several decades of writing medical research documents, Cindy Dorminy decided to switch gears and become an author. She wanted to write stories where the chances of happy endings are 100% and the side effects include satisfied sighs, permanent smiles, and a chuckle or two.

Cindy was born in Texas and raised in Georgia. She enjoys gardening, reading, and bodybuilding. She can often be overheard quoting lines from her favorite movies. But her favorite pastime is spending time with Mark, her bass-playing husband, and Maddie Rose, the coolest girl on the planet. She also loves her fur child, Daisy Mae. She currently resides in Nashville, TN, where live music can be heard everywhere, even at the grocery store.

Read more at www.cindydwrites.com.

About the Publisher

Dear Reader,

We hope you enjoyed this book. Please consider leaving a review on your favorite book site.

Visit https://RedAdeptPublishing.com to see our entire catalogue.

Check out our app for short stories, articles, and interviews. You'll also be notified of future releases and special sales.